LIZ FIELDING
Wedded in a Whirlwind

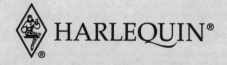

HARLEQUIN®

TORONTO • NEW YORK • LONDON
AMSTERDAM • PARIS • SYDNEY • HAMBURG
STOCKHOLM • ATHENS • TOKYO • MILAN • MADRID
PRAGUE • WARSAW • BUDAPEST • AUCKLAND

ISBN-13: 978-0-373-17548-2
ISBN-10: 0-373-17548-5

WEDDED IN A WHIRLWIND

First North American Publication 2008.

Copyright © 2008 by Liz Fielding.

This edition published by arrangement with Harlequin Books S.A.

® and TM are trademarks of the publisher. Trademarks indicated with ® are registered in the United States Patent and Trademark Office, the Canadian Trade Marks Office and in other countries.

www.eHarlequin.com

Printed in U.S.A.

don't need you to get me out of here." And she continued to kick and writhe until she connected solidly with his shin.

It was enough. The girl was slender, but she had a kick like a mule, and he rolled over, pinning her to the ground.

"Be still," he warned, abandoning reassurance, making it an order. He'd have to let go to slap her, and while the temptation was almost overwhelming—he was still feeling that kick—he chose the only other alternative left open to him, and kissed her.

It was brutal, but effective, cutting off the stream of invectives, cutting off her breath, and, taken by surprise, she went rigid beneath him. And then, just as swiftly, she was clinging to him, her mouth hot and eager as she pressed against him, desperate for the warmth of a human body. For comfort in the darkness. A no-holds-barred kiss. Pure, honest, raw need that tapped into something deep inside him.

As suddenly as it had begun, it was over. Miranda slumped back against the cracked and now sloping floor of the temple.

"Don't! Don't ever do that again!"

"I could just as easily have slapped you," he said.

In truth they were both breathing rather more heavily, and her verbal rejection was certainly not being followed up by her body. Or his. Being this close to a woman who was no more than curves that fit his body like a glove, soft skin, a scent in the darkness, was doing something to his head.

Dear Reader,

One of the joys of writing is the moment when you recognize that a character you've created to fill a supporting role in one book has taken on an importance, a presence, that makes her a natural heroine.

It happened when I wrote *A Wife on Paper* and Matty Lang wheeled herself onto the page, a heroine so wonderful that she won herself a RITA® Award for *The Marriage Miracle*.

Last year, when Miranda Grenville—difficult, flawed, fragile—played her part in *Reunited: Marriage in a Million,* I knew that she had a story to tell. She had a secret so terrible that she'd never shared it with anyone, not even her brother.

Her story begins when, desperate to escape an overabundance of happy-ever-afters, she takes the first holiday destination she's offered and flies to the new resort island of Cordillera. It rapidly turns into a nightmare, but sparring with Matt Jago—a man who gives as good as he gets—certainly livens things up, and they swiftly learn to trust and respect the other's strengths. Then, in their darkest moment, they spill out secrets never before shared with anyone, learning to leave the past behind them and reach for a new beginning.

But can the fierce intensity of their brief relationship survive in the real world? Will this whirlwind romance become a lifetime of love?

I'll leave you to find out.

With love,

Liz

Liz Fielding was born with itchy feet. She made it to Zambia before her twenty-first birthday and, gathering her own special hero and a couple of children on the way, lived in Botswana, Kenya and Bahrain—with pauses for sightseeing pretty much everywhere in between. She finally came to a full stop in a tiny Welsh village cradled by misty hills, and these days she mostly leaves her pen to do the traveling. When she's not sorting out the lives and loves of her characters, she potters in the garden, reads her favorite authors and spends a lot of time wondering "What if…?" For news of upcoming books—and to sign up for her occasional newsletter—visit Liz's Web site at www.lizfielding.com.

CHAPTER ONE

MIRANDA GRENVILLE stood through the double baptism, holding each baby in turn as she made the promises, heard the vicar name names…

Minette Daisy…

Jude Michael…

Stood with each glowing mother—first her sister-in-law, Belle, and then Belle's sister, Daisy—smiling as everyone took photographs. Even took some herself.

It was, without doubt, the most joyous occasion and her smile never faltered despite the turmoil of feelings that, inside, were tearing her apart.

Keeping her emotions hidden had been a hard-learned lesson, far more difficult than anything that came out of books; books were easy. But when, finally, the pain had become so great that hiding it had become essential for survival she had found the strength from somewhere.

It hadn't always been like that.

There had been a time when she had let everything show, let her emotional need hang out for all the world to see. It had been a slow and painful lesson—one she'd learned from watching Ivo, her brother. She'd thought he was immune, but the power of a love that was beyond her comprehension, the joy of fatherhood, had shattered the ice cage that once held her brother a fellow prisoner in emotional stasis. Now she was isolated, bound and shackled by the one secret she had never shared with a living soul—not even with Ivo.

And so she smiled for him on this joyous day. Not that he was fooled. He knew her too well for that. Recognised her smile for the brittle thing that it was, sensing a fragility beneath the controlled veneer.

To see his puzzled watchfulness, his anxiety for her, clouding his eyes on what should have been the happiest of days made her feel like the spectre at the feast. She had to get away before he sought her out and asked the question she could see in his eyes.

Is there something I can do?

The answer was—had to be—no. He had already done more than enough. He'd been there with the tough as well as the tender love. He had been her lifeline, keeping her afloat, even when she'd come close to dragging him under with her.

He had a new life now and it was time to cut the ties, set him free of all that chained him to a painful past. She had to convince him that she didn't need him any more, so she smiled until her face ached, toasted the babies, snapped pictures on her cellphone, tasted a crumb of each christening cake.

She was on the point of breaking when her sister-in-law announced that Minette needing feeding and she seized her chance.

'Belle, I have to go,' she said, following her into the nursery.

'So soon?' Belle took her hand, not to detain her, but in a gesture that was utterly natural to her, full of warmth, a kindness she knew she didn't deserve. She had bitterly resented the glamorous Belle Davenport's intrusion into her brother's life. She'd hated her for being the kind of woman who drew people to her, hated her because Ivo couldn't live without her, and she'd gone out of her way to make her feel like an outsider in her own home. Drive her away.

Stupid.

She, of all people, should have known that, once given, Ivo's love was unshakeable.

'I've got a plane to catch,' she said, moving away. She didn't want or need kindness. Didn't deserve it. 'It's been a hectic few months researching the documentary on adoption and I thought I'd take the opportunity to grab some time for myself before we start filming.'

While Belle and Daisy were taking maternity leave from the television production company the three of them ran as a team.

'What bliss,' Belle said. 'Anywhere interesting?'

'Somewhere without a telephone,' she replied. The caustic edge to her voice had become as natural as breathing. Actually it wasn't such a bad idea. Then, as Minette searched hungrily for her mother's breast and began to suckle, the sharp, woman-of-the-world act buckled and she had to look away. 'Tell Ivo for me, will you?' she asked through a throat that was thickening dangerously. 'And Daisy.'

'You're not going to say goodbye?'

'It's better if I just slip away.' She managed a shrug. 'You know what Ivo's like.' He'd see right through her. 'He'll want to know where I'm going. Make me promise to keep in touch.'

A promise she couldn't keep.

She needed to get away completely. Give him space to enjoy his new family. Escape from an excess of consideration, warmth, kindness and go somewhere where no one knew her. Where she could stop smiling, be angry, be herself…

About to say something, her sister-in-law changed her mind, instead squeezing her hand. 'Thank you, Manda.'

'What for? I promise you're going to regret inviting me to

be Minette's godmother. I plan to set both my godchildren a thoroughly bad example.'

Belle shook her head, not taking her in the least bit seriously. 'Not just for being Minette's godmother, but for being so brilliant with Daisy, giving her a job, a purpose when she most needed it.'

'I wouldn't have kept her on if she hadn't proved her worth,' she lied.

She'd taken on Belle's damaged little sister for her brother's sake, her attempt to atone a little for the hurt she'd caused him, make amends, but in truth she understood Daisy in ways that Belle never could. She'd been in the same dark places, knew what worked and what didn't, had known how to be tough when Belle had been emotionally racked.

'Just warn Daisy from me that if she has any idea of becoming a stay-at-home mother she'd better think again,' she said, sidestepping the soft-centred mush. 'I've spent too much time training her in my little ways to let her off the hook.'

'And thank you for not making a fuss when Ivo sold the house,' Belle continued, refusing to be distracted from saying exactly what was on her mind. 'I know how hard that must have been for you.'

Hard…

The Belgravia mansion that had been in her family for generations—a backdrop for the financial and political dinners, receptions, she'd arranged for her brother—had been her whole life when she didn't have a life and she'd lavished all she had in the way of love on its care.

Belle, who'd hated the house from the minute she'd stepped over the threshold, hadn't the faintest idea how hard it had been to let it go, but still, with a throat that ached and a heart like lead, Manda held her smile.

'It would be a bit big for one.' Then, 'I've got to go.'

'Manda…'

'Now,' she said, turning away and heading for the door before Belle did something stupid, like hug her. Before the tears stinging her eyelids spilled over and the ice cool image, the touch-me-not façade she'd built so carefully over the last few years cracked and she made a total fool of herself.

Nick Jago slid on to a stool and the barman, a leathery Australian whose yacht had been wrecked off the coast of Cordillera ten years earlier and had never found the energy to move on, poured him a small cup of thick black coffee and pushed it across the counter.

'It's a while since you were in town,' he said.

'I just came in to pick up my mail. There isn't much else to tempt me into what passes for civilisation around here.'

'Maybe not, but stuck out there by yourself you tend to miss the news.' He produced a month-old copy of an English newspaper from beneath the counter. 'I hung on to this for you.'

Jago glanced at the headlines of a tabloid that had the nerve to call itself a newspaper. Another politician caught with his pants down. Another family torn apart.

'No, thanks, Rob,' he said. 'I'm not that desperate for something to read.'

'Not that,' he replied dismissively. 'Inside. There's a picture that I think'll interest you.'

'And you can keep your page three girls. Fliss will be back soon and I'd rather wait for the real thing.'

'You sure about that?'

He shrugged. He was sure of nothing but death, taxes, and that her goodbye had been accompanied by a hot, lingering kiss that had been better than any promise. But Rob clearly knew something he didn't.

'Why do I have the feeling you're about to disillusion me?'

'I hate to be the bearer of bad news, mate,' Rob replied, 'but I have to tell you that your Fliss might have other things on her mind.' He opened the paper at a double page spread. *"Sex, Slavery and Sacrifice... Exclusive excerpts from the sensational diaries of beautiful archaeologist Fliss Grant..."*', he read out loud.

Jago, his cup halfway to his mouth, slowly returned it to its saucer.

Archaeologist?

She'd been a postgrad student when she'd turned up at his dig. A volunteer, working for food and experience. There were a hundred more like her—well, maybe not exactly like her—but he wouldn't have paid her, no matter how hot her kisses.

Rob, under the mistaken impression that he wanted to hear more, continued.

'"Discover the secrets of Cordillera's long lost Temple of Fire. Win a holiday on this exotic island paradise and see for yourself the ancient sacrificial stone—"'

'What?'

Jago grabbed the paper.

One look at the photograph of the sexy blonde, one look at her khaki shirt, held together only by a knot beneath generous breasts and exposing a lot more flesh than the average archaeological assistant would sensibly display on a hard day at a dig, was enough.

Not that Fliss Grant was average in any way.

He hadn't heard from her since she'd left the island at the end of the digging season when the rains had set in, but then he hadn't expected to. There was no mobile phone signal up in the hills.

He hadn't been bothered—honesty compelled him to admit that conversation had never been the attraction—and he'd had plenty of other things to keep him occupied.

As for the Cordilleran postal service—well, even if she had been moved to write, it was something of a hit-or-miss affair. It was why, when she'd offered to deliver copies of disks containing his diaries and photographs to his publisher, he'd handed them over without a second thought.

He stared at the photograph.

The very brief shorts, a slick sheen of sweat, the wet-look lips and provocative pose had been used to set the tone for diaries written '... *by this dauntless female "Indiana Jones" who braved spiders, scorpions and deadly snakes to uncover the secrets of the island's mysterious past...*'

There was a photograph of a large hairy spider to ram the message home.

'*I knew the temples were there...*'—She knew!—'*...and I was determined to prove it. Now you can read for yourself what I had to endure to discover the terrible truth behind the sacrificial stone...*'

'Give me strength,' he muttered as he attempted to get his head around what he was seeing. And then, when he did, something painful squeezed at his chest and his mouth dried. She hadn't simply taken the chance to make a heap of money using his diaries, his work.

He could have understood the temptation and, wrapped in her hot thighs, he might even have forgiven her. But there was another smaller photograph of Fliss and Felipe Dominez, Cordillera's playboy Minister of Tourism, snapped as they'd left one of London's fashionable nightclubs. She was wearing a dress that left little to the imagination and they were ex-changing the kind of intimate look shared only by two people who knew one another very well.

So the only question left unanswered was when had Dominez and Fliss met?

Had it been by chance on one of her little excursions into town for supplies? Had Dominez sought her out and made her an offer she couldn't possibly refuse?

Or had he been set up from the very start?

It wasn't that unusual for postgraduate archaeology students to turn up out of the blue, having paid their own way to the site. They needed field experience to boost their CVs and he needed all the help he could get. The fact that Fliss Grant had a mouth, a body, as hot as sin that she'd been willing and eager to share with him had just made having her around that much more pleasurable.

No, he decided. This hadn't been chance. The speed with which she'd achieved publication suggested that it was the cul-mination of a well thought out and efficiently executed plan.

Fliss Grant, it seemed, had 'endured' and 'endured' in order to get her hands on his diaries, his notes, his photographs and why would he be surprised by that? Women, as he was well aware, would endure anything to get what they wanted.

Not that she'd actually used any direct quotes, but then why would she bother? This publishing venture had nothing to do with dry scholarship.

He had no doubt that some hack, paid by Dominez, had ghosted this fairy tale from the bones of his excavation diaries, just as someone had been paid to make sketches from his photographs, producing an impression of the temple complex peopled with priests and sacrificial figures that had more in common with a fifties Hollywood epic than reality.

Not that he'd been credited in any way.

From this account, anyone would think Fliss had exca-vated the temple single-handed, enough to warn anyone with an atom of common sense that this was all hokum. But then this was straight out of the 'God was an astronaut' school of archaeology.

As he scanned the prurient accounts of priestly rites, he knew he should be grateful that his name had been omitted from this tabloid version of the temple's history with its sexed-up versions of the images carved into the stone walls. The 'naked virgins', 'bloody sacrifice' scenarios, the sexual innu-endo, were not something he'd want his name attached to.

But somehow, at that moment, gratitude of any kind was beyond him. This rubbish would reduce him to a laughing stock within the academic archaeological world and, without a word, he reached for the bottle of local brandy that Rob pushed in his direction.

It was unbelievably hot. No temple, no matter how ancient, was worth this kind of suffering, Manda decided, wiping the back of her arm across her forehead to mop up the sweat.

'Come along, keep up,' the guide called, with an imperi-ous gesture. 'There's a lot more to see.'

He was evidently new to the job and hadn't quite got the customer service thing nailed.

Since rebellion in the ranks was apparently unthinkable, he didn't wait to ensure that he was obeyed but plunged further along the path in the direction of yet more ruins, his charges meekly trailing after him. Well, most of them.

Manda was not meek. Far from it. And she'd already had enough of this particular ancient civilisation to last her a lifetime.

Refusing to move another yard, she sank on to a huge

fallen chunk of dressed stone that someone, long ago, had started to chisel into a representation of some beast. He'd evidently given up halfway through his task and if it had been a day like this, he had her sympathy.

She leaned forward, unfastening another button of a limp linen shirt that had not been designed for this kind of sweaty exertion, flapping the two edges to encourage what air there was to circulate and cool her damp skin.

Next time she grabbed the first flight on offer to the Far East, she'd take more notice of where she was going. Cordillera, she'd been assured when she'd called the booking agency, was going to be the next 'big' destination. She had caught part of a chat show interview with some impossibly glamorous female archaeologist who'd written a book about how she'd personally—and apparently entirely unaided—uncovered some ancient civilisation on the island, so maybe it was true.

Not really her thing; she'd been more interested in promises of unspoiled palm-fringed coves and white sand. Unspoiled was a euphemism for a lack of amenities, she discovered. They were trying, but the 'resort' at which she was staying was, so far, little more than a construction site.

Normally one look would have been enough. She'd have turned right around and caught the next plane out of there, flown on to somewhere where luxury was guaranteed.

But she'd cut and run from feelings she couldn't handle, had told herself she didn't care where she was going and, having stuck the equivalent of a metaphorical pin in the map, fate had brought her here.

Maybe this was fate's idea of a joke but it had fulfilled a major part of her desire to be out of contact and its awfulness had, somehow, seemed exactly right.

But the lack of facilities, and an airport blockbuster that hadn't lived up to its blurb, had left her bored enough to break the habit of a lifetime and allow herself to be persuaded by a representative from the tourist office, eager to promote the island, that it was something of a privilege to be one of the first outsiders to see the ruins. A real adventure. Something she'd tell all her friends about when she got home.

She hadn't been totally convinced but at the time anything had seemed better than sitting alone with nothing but her thoughts for company.

Big mistake, she thought, pushing back damp strands of hair that were sticking to her forehead and pulling a face. Unfortunately, thirty miles inland, halfway up the side of a mountain on a route march around the seemingly endless maze of what they had been assured were the ancient temples and palaces, it was too late to change her mind.

Jago had been sitting on the altar stone for what felt like hours still holding the bottle of local brandy that Rob had slid across the bar, muttering, 'On the house, mate…'

One more season was all he'd needed and then, come the next rains, he'd have returned to London and published his findings in the academic journals. Written a book that would never have made the bestseller list. There was nothing here sensational enough for that. No treasure. No startling revelations.

He wasn't interested in sensationalism, bestseller lists, anything that would expose him to the glare of celebrity. If he'd wanted them, they could have been his for the asking any time in the last fifteen years.

All he'd wanted was to drop out of sight and lose himself in the work he loved.

He looked down at the bottle in his hand and finally broke the seal.

* * *

For a while Manda remained where she was, perched on her stone, quite content to wait until the rest of her party returned, idly tracing the outline of the half-finished figure with the tip of her finger. It was the head of a bird, she realised, a hawk of some kind, and she glanced up at a sky almost crowded out by the thick canopy of the forest.

When their pitiful little band of tourists—a couple of dozen people who were staying at the same complex, boosted by a group of captive businessmen whose plane had been delayed—had walked up from a clearing where they'd left the bus, she'd noticed a hawk, its wings outstretched and seemingly motionless as it rode the currents of air, quartering the side of the valley in search of prey.

She searched the small patch of sky that was now streaked with pink, but the bird had gone and the forest was wonderfully peaceful. She could no longer hear the tour guide's sing-song voice pointing out the details they were expected to admire enthusiastically when, in truth, all they'd wanted was to be back at the coast with a very cold drink within easy reach.

She sipped at the bottle of water she carried in her shoulder bag before pouring a small amount on to the hem of her shirt to wipe over her face. Then, wondering how much longer she would have to endure this 'privilege', she glanced at her watch.

Three o'clock? Was that all it was?

She frowned. The pink streaks in the sky suggested it was later. She'd reset her watch to local time when she'd landed, but maybe she'd got it wrong; she hadn't actually been paying much attention to the time.

She stared up at the sky for a moment longer, then at the path taken by her companions. Night fell with stunning rapidity in this part of the world and she listened for any sound that might indicate their imminent return.

There was nothing. The birds had fallen silent, the insects had stopped their apparently ceaseless stridulating as if they, too, were listening.

The absolute quiet that a minute or two earlier had seemed so welcome now seemed strangely eerie, prickling her skin with goose-flesh, setting up the small hairs on the back of her neck at some unseen, unknown danger. A feeling that the earth itself was holding its breath.

'Wait!' Her urgent cry seemed pathetically small, smothered by the density of the vegetation and, in a sudden burst of panic at the thought of being left on her own in that ancient, ghost-filled place, she leapt to her feet and, quite oblivious of the heat, began to scramble up the steep path after the others.

'Wait,' she cried out again. 'Wait for me.'

She had covered perhaps twenty yards when she staggered slightly and, stumbling, put her hand to the ground to save herself. She didn't stop to wonder at such unaccustomed clumsiness, she was in too much of a hurry to catch up with the rest of the party. Then, as she took another step, she lost her balance again and grabbed for a tree as she was overcome with dizziness, staring down at the forest floor, which appeared to be rippling beneath her feet. Puzzled, but not yet alarmed.

Leaves, small pieces of twig and bark began to tumble from the dense canopy high above her and she gave a startled little scream as something hit her shoulder and bounced to the ground. It was a large spider and, for a moment, they stared at one another, both of them confused by the earth's uncharacteristic behaviour. Then the tree she was clinging to began to shake and Manda forgot all about the spider.

For a moment she hung on, clinging to the thick trunk regardless of the debris raining down on her head and shoulders, unable to concentrate on anything but the absolute necessity of remaining on her feet as the earth shook.

If she could just hold on, it would stop and then she would walk slowly back down the path to the tour bus and wait for the others to return.

Except that it didn't.

Instead, the shaking grew steadily worse until the ground beneath her felt as if it were surging in great undulating waves and the tree she was clinging on to for dear life lurched sideways as the path split open with a great jagged tear.

For a frozen moment in time Manda hung on, staring down into the thick green forest that carpeted the valley wall rippling beneath her like some storm-tossed sea. Then, as she realised she was about to be tipped into that maelstrom, she let go of the tree and flung herself across the gaping path a split second before the tree, its roots and the ground to which they were attached, fell away like a stone.

She was screaming now. Seriously screaming.

She knew she was screaming because, although she could not hear herself—all she could hear was the crack and roar as the earth split and tore about her—she could feel the harsh vibration in her throat.

Lying where she had thrown herself in her mad leap for safety, her arms wrapped around her head, her eyes tightly closed, she shrieked, 'Enough! No more, God. Stop it! Please!'

Then the ground beneath her gave way and she, too, was sliding into the abyss.

CHAPTER TWO

MANDA had no way of knowing what time it was, or how long she had been lying on cold stone. She was just grateful that the earth had stopped shaking.

After a while, though, she lifted her head, gingerly feeling for damage. Her fingers were stiff, sore as she tried to move them and there was a tender spot at the back of her head. A dull throbbing ache. Nothing that she couldn't, for the moment, live with, she decided. And she seemed lucid enough.

Lucid enough to know that she had lived through an earthquake and be grateful to have survived.

Lucid enough to know that living through the initial catastrophe might not be enough. She had been alone, separated from her party…

She let her head fall back against the stone and lay still for a moment while she gathered her wits, her strength, knowing that she should move, shout, do something to make herself heard, alert searchers to her presence.

In a moment.

She would do all that in a moment.

It was dark. Pitch-dark. There were no stars, no moon, which suggested dense cloud cover. Was that normal after earthquakes? Tropical rain would be the absolute limit, she thought, as she tried to piece together exactly what had happened.

The earth shaking. The path splitting. Her fingers clawing at the earth as she had begun to fall.

She went cold as she relived that moment of terror as she'd been carried down on a torrent of earth and stones. As she realised just what that meant. Why there was no sky.

It wasn't cloud that was blocking it out. She'd fallen into some cavity. Into one of the temples? Maybe even one that hadn't been excavated. Or even discovered…

She was beneath the ground. Buried. Entombed. Locked in…

Panic sucked the breath from her. Her cry was wordless and, while every instinct was urging her to fling herself at the walls, claw her way out, she was unable to move.

She knew this feeling. The claustrophobia. The desperation to escape. Her body and mind too numb to do anything about it.

She'd been here before.

She swallowed hard, forced herself to concentrate on breathing…

In. One, two, three…

Told herself that it wasn't the same.

Hold. One, two, three…

That had been a mental lockdown. She'd been confined by the darkness in her mind.

Out. One, two, three…

This was physical.

She could do something about this, dig herself out with her bare hands if need be, she told herself, even as she strained desperately for the comfort of voices, the clink of stones being turned. A promise that there was someone there. A hand in the darkness.

There was nothing. Only a blanketing silence. Only the rapid beating of her pulse in her ears.

For a moment she lost the rhythm of her breathing, gasping for air as fear began to overwhelm her.

She couldn't afford to panic. It would be a waste of energy, a waste of time, and if there was one thing she'd learned, it was how to take control of her body, her emotions.

Breathe in to the count of three…

She had to shut down everything but the core need to concentrate.

Hold to the count of three…

After that she could make a careful assessment of her situation. Decide what action to take. If ever there was a time to use everything she'd learned—to block out emotion by fixing on what had to be done, making a plan and carrying it through, this was it. If she once succumbed to mind-numbing, will-sapping terror…

Easier said than done.

Control was easy when you were calling all the shots, when you were the one directing events. But it was a long time since she'd been thrown entirely on her own resources.

In the metaphorical dark.

At least this dark was physical. Not that it was much comfort. She was miles from anywhere and even if any of her party was capable of making it to the nearest village it would take time for help to arrive.

She blotted that out.

She mustn't think about that.

Breathe, breathe… The air, at least, was fresh. For now.

She tried to swallow but her throat was dry. There was water in her bag. She had to find her bag. Concentrate on what she could do to keep herself alive because it was far too soon for any serious attempt at rescue.

If she was ever going to get out of here, the important thing was to keep calm. Conserve her strength.

She listened for the smallest sound.

The silence was so dense that it was like a suffocating weight against her eardrums, her chest and once again it almost overwhelmed her and she had to force herself to focus on normal, everyday things. Good things.

Ivo and Belle.

Daisy.

The precious new babies...

At least they didn't know where she was. Wouldn't be glued to news reports, worrying themselves sick. Ivo wouldn't be flying here to take charge...

No. On second thoughts that didn't help. She needed someone out there moving heaven and earth to find her. Lots of earth and stone.

But it wasn't going to happen.

She'd cut loose, broken the ties, had wanted to prove that she was capable of standing of her own feet.

Great timing, Manda...

Maybe she should see if she could stand up, try exploring her surroundings. Maybe she could find her own way out.

'See' being the operative word.

Alone in the dark, it was as if she had suddenly been struck blind and deaf. She lifted a hand but couldn't see it until it was right in front of her face and even then she wasn't sure if she could actually see it, or whether her brain was providing a picture of what she knew was there.

She'd never been in such absolute darkness, the kind of

darkness that made an overcast night in the depths of Norfolk seem bright as day.

Maybe, she thought, with a rising tide of panic, she really was blind. Or deaf. Or both. Maybe she'd banged her head harder than she'd imagined and lost those precious vital senses. Maybe she'd been unconscious for hours.

In a sudden desperate need to remind herself that this wasn't so, she shouted, 'Help!'

Trapped in the confined space, her voice echoed and reverberated back at her, again and again until she covered her ears.

There was nothing wrong with her hearing.

She was just alone and in the dark. It might be her worst nightmare, but she wasn't about to wake up and find Ivo waiting to pick up the pieces and put her back together again. Not this time.

There would be no Belle to reach wordlessly for her hand.

No Daisy to grin at her, say something utterly outrageous.

A groan escaped her and suddenly her precious lucidity did not seem such a prize.

Muddle-headed, her memory would not be quite so painfully sharp. Confused, she wouldn't be quite so aware of the danger of her position.

Fear, real icy-cold fear, began to seep into every pore as she realised that, separated from her companions, no one would even know where to begin looking for her...

'Shut up, Manda,' she said. Then tried to decide whether talking to herself was a good sign or a bad one.

Rubbing briskly at her arms, she made a determined effort to exclude the building terror by thinking of something else.

Working out exactly where she was.

Okay.

She'd been standing on a forest path, so logic suggested

that she should now be buried beneath tons of earth and vegetation. But she wasn't. Which was a good thing.

Instead, she was in a dark, echoing space, which presumably meant she had fallen into one of the temples.

Which was not...

The path had twisted and turned as they had climbed up the side of the hill and she tried to remember the temple they had visited before she had rebelled against so much enforced culture. Tried to remember which way the path had turned, but the darkness was confusing, blocking her thoughts.

If only she could see!

'Stop it, Miranda Grenville,' she told herself sternly. So she couldn't see. Tough. For her it was just a temporary inconvenience. There were millions of people who were forced to live with it every day of their lives. They coped and so would she.

Her eyes would adapt to the darkness in a few minutes.

She'd get herself out of there...

She stopped the thought before it reached the inevitable... *if it was the last thing she did.*

There was no point in tempting fate. Fate, it was clear, was already on her case in a big way. She had to treat this as if it were some organisational problem. The kind she'd handled for Ivo every day of her working life until she'd made the move to set up her own television production company with Belle and Daisy. Proving to herself, to everyone, that she no longer needed her brother as a prop.

Except that so far it had been a one-show wonder and without Belle...

No! Belle was brilliant in front of the camera, but she was the one who'd made it happen. That was what she did. Give her a goal, a project to bring in on time and she'd deliver the goods and she'd get herself out of here, too.

Breathe!

One, two, three…

Get up!

Rubble rattled off her as she finally managed to sit up; small pieces of stone, along with what felt like half a ton of fine cloying dust that rose up to choke her.

Coughing as the dust filled her nose, her throat, filtered down into her sensitive bronchial passages, Manda groped around for her bag. She'd been holding on to it as she'd taken off after the rest of the party and it must have fallen through the gap in the earth with her, although obviously not conveniently at her side.

Her left arm buckled a little as she eased herself forward to spread her arc of search, her elbow giving way when she put weight on it. Prompted by this, all her other joints decided to join in. Her left knee began to throb. Her shoulder. Her fingers were already stinging…

She stopped making a mental inventory when she realised that she hurt pretty much everywhere and instead congratulated herself that nothing seemed to be broken, although she hadn't actually tried to stand up yet. She flexed her toes but nothing too bad happened.

She had, it seemed, been lucky.

The last thing she remembered was the ground heaving upwards, shifting sideways, tipping her through into the earth's basement like so much garbage, but at least she was in one piece and able to move about.

Check out her surroundings…

She spread her hands and began to feel around for her bag. That had to be her first priority. She had water in her bag.

No luck.

She carefully eased herself to her knees, then cautiously

to her feet, feeling above her for the roof, blinking rapidly as if that would somehow clear her vision.

Her hands met no resistance, but maybe her eyes had adjusted a little because the darkness didn't seem quite so dense now. Or were those shapes no more than her brain playing tricks?

She swallowed, inched forward, hands outstretched, letting out a tiny shriek as her palms touched something. For a moment her heart went into overdrive, even while her head processed the information.

Cold, flat. It was a wall.

Once she'd regained her breath, she began to edge her way carefully around the boundary of her underground prison.

She was certain now that she was in one of the temples. They had passed a truly impressive entrance that had been more thoroughly cleared than the rest, but the guide had hurried them past, nervously warning that it was 'not safe' when one of the businessmen had stopped, wanting to go inside.

At the time she hadn't questioned it; she'd just been grateful to be spared yet more of the same. But, before they'd been hurried on, she had glimpsed tools of some kind, a work table.

The tools would be very welcome right now. And if someone was working there, presumably there'd be a lamp, water...

She tried not to think about what would happen if she didn't find her bag with her water bottle. She'd find it...

Every now and then her fingers encountered sharply cut images carved into the walls. Protected from the elements within the temple walls, they were as clean-edged as the day they had been chiselled into the stone.

She had seen enough of them before she'd abandoned the tour and her brain, deprived of light, eagerly supplied pictures of those strange stylised creatures to fill the void.

In the powerful beam of the guide's torch they had seemed slightly sinister.

In the blackness her imagination amplified the threat and she began to shiver.

Stupid, stupid…

Concentrate. Breathe…

She counted the steps around the edge of her cell. Two, three, four… Her mind refused to co-operate but took itself off on a diversion to wonder about her companions. Had they survived? Were they, even now, being picked up by some rescue team? Would they realise that she wasn't with them?

One of the businessmen had been eyeing her with a great deal more interest than the ruins. Maybe he would alert the rescuers to her absence. Assuming there were any rescuers.

Assuming any of them had survived.

That thought brought the fear seeping back and for a moment she leaned against the wall as a great shuddering sigh swept through her and she covered her ears as if to block it out.

There was no point in dwelling on such negative thoughts. She had to keep strong, in control, to survive. But, even as she clung to that thought, the wall began to shake.

'No!' She didn't know whether she screamed it out loud or whether the agonised word was a whisper in her mind as an aftershock flung her away from its illusory protection.

She used her hands to protect herself, landing painfully on palms and knees.

Dust showered down on to her, filling her eyes and, as she gasped for air, her mouth. For a moment she was certain she was about to suffocate and in sheer terror she let rip with a scream.

That was when, out of the darkness, fingers clamped tightly about her arm and a gravelly voice said, 'For pity's sake, woman, give it a rest…'

CHAPTER THREE

JAGO appeared to have the hangover from hell, which was odd. Getting drunk would have been an understandable reaction to the discovery that Fliss had been using him and he'd certainly had the means, thanks to Rob. But he was fairly certain that, on reflection, he'd decided he'd taken enough punishment for one day.

Or maybe that was simply wishful thinking because there was no doubt that right now he was lying with his face pressed against the cold stone of the floor. Not a good sign. And he was hurting pretty much everywhere but mostly inside his head, where an incompetent but unbelievably enthusiastic drummer was using his skull for practice.

He would have told him to stop, but it was too much trouble.

That was the problem with drinking to forget. While it might seem like a great idea when you were swallowing the hot local liquor that offered instant oblivion, unfortunately it was a temporary state unless you kept on drinking.

He remembered thinking that as the first mouthful had burned its way down his throat and then…

And then nothing.

Dumber than he'd thought, then, and come morning he'd be sorry he hadn't made the effort to make it as far as the camp-bed, but what was one more regret? He'd scarcely notice it amongst the pile already waiting to be sifted through.

Right now, what he needed was water and he groped around him, hoping to find a bottle within reach. Aspirin would be good too, but that was going to have to wait until he'd recovered a little.

His fingers encountered rubble.

Rubble?

Where on earth was he?

His forehead creased in a frown which he instantly regretted, swearing silently as the pain drilled through his skull. It didn't take a genius to work out that if a simple frown caused that kind of grief, anything louder than a thought would be unwise.

He closed his eyes and, for the moment, the pain in his head receded a little. But only for a moment. The ground, it seemed, had other ideas, refusing to leave him in peace, shaking him like a dog at a bone. And, if that wasn't bad enough, there was some woman having hysterics practically in his ear.

Oblivion was a lot harder to come by than you'd think.

He turned over, reached out and, as his palm connected with smooth, firm flesh he wondered, without too much interest, who she was. Before growling at her to shut up.

There was a startled yelp and then blissful silence. And the earth had finally stopped making a fuss too.

A result.

He let his head fall back against the floor.

It was too good to last.

'Hello?' The woman's voice, now she'd stopped screaming, was low, a little bit husky, with the kind of catch in it that would undoubtedly ensnare any poor sap who hadn't already learned the hard way that no woman was ever that vulnerable.

It wasn't that he was immune. Far from it.

He might be feeling awful, but his body still automatically tightened in hopeful response to the enticing warmth of a woman's voice up close in the dark.

It was over-optimistic.

A grunt was, for the moment, the limit of his ambition but he forced open unwilling eyelids and lifted his head an inch or two to take a look.

Opening his eyes didn't make much difference, he discovered, but since light would have only added to his pain he decided to be grateful for small mercies. But not that grateful. Women were definitely off the agenda and he said, 'Clear off.'

Having got that off his chest, he closed his eyes and let his head drop back to the floor.

'Wh-who are you?' She might be nervous but she was irritatingly persistent. 'Are you hurt?'

'Terminally,' he assured her. 'Body and soul. Totally beyond saving, so do me a favour. Go away and leave me to die in peace.'

No chance. She was a woman so she did the opposite, moving closer, finding his shoulder, feeling for his neck. She was checking his pulse, he realised. The stupid female had taken him seriously...

Apparently satisfied that he wasn't, despite his protestations, about to expire on her, she slid her hand up to his cheek, laying long cool fingers against it, soothing his pounding head which, if he were honest, he had to admit felt pretty good.

'Who are you?' she persisted, her voice stronger now that she'd satisfied herself that he was in one piece. In fact, she had the crisp enunciation of a woman who expected an answer. Without delay.

Her touch wasn't *that* good.

Delete vulnerable and caring, replace with bossy, interfering, typical of a particular type of organising female with whom he was very familiar. The ones he knew all had moustaches and chaired committees that allocated research funding...

He didn't bother to answer. She didn't give up but leaned over him so that he was assailed by the musky scent of warm skin before, after a pause, she wiped something damp over his face.

'Is that better?' she asked.

He was getting very mixed messages here, but provided she kept the volume down she could carry on with her Florence Nightingale act.

'Were you on the bus?' she asked.

Jago sighed.

That was the trouble with women; they couldn't be content with just doing the ministering angel stuff. They had to talk. Worse, they insisted you answer them.

'Don't you understand simple English?' he growled, swatting away her hand. The price of comfort came too high.

She didn't take the hint, but laid it over his forehead in a way that suggested she thought he might not be entirely right in it. The head, that was. Definitely one of the moustache brigade, he thought, although her hand had the soft, pampered feel of someone who took rather more care of her appearance. Soft and pampered and her long, caressing fingers were giving his body ideas whether his head was coming along for the ride or not.

Definitely not yet another archaeology student looking for postgrad experience, then. At least that was something in her favour. Not even Fliss, who had lavished cream on every part of her body—generously inviting him to lend a hand—had been able to keep her hands entirely callus-free.

But she *was* female, so that cancelled out all the plus points. Including that warm female scent that a man, if he was dumb enough, could very easily lose himself in...

'Read my lips,' he said, snapping back from temptation. 'Go away.'

'I can't see your damn lips,' she replied sharply. The mild expletive sounded unexpectedly shocking when spoken in that expensive finishing school accent.

And she didn't move.

On the contrary, she dropped her head so that her hair brushed against his cheek. He recognised the scent now. Rosemary.

It was rosemary.

His mother had planted a bush by the garden gate. Some superstitious nonsense was involved, he seemed to remember. It had grown over the path so that he'd brushed against it when he wheeled out his bike...

This woman used rosemary-scented shampoo and it took him right back to memories he thought he'd buried too deep to ever be dredged up again and he told her, this time in the most basic of terms, to go away.

'Can you move?' she asked, ignoring him. 'Where does it hurt?'

Woman, thy name is persistence...

'What I've got is a headache,' he said. 'You.' He thought about sitting up but not very seriously. 'I don't suppose you've come across a bottle around here by any chance?'

Since she insisted on staying, she might as well make herself useful.

'Bottle?' She sniffed. Then the soft hand was snatched back from his forehead. 'You're drunk!' she exclaimed.

Unlikely. Headache notwithstanding, he was, unhappily, thinking far too clearly for it to be alcohol-related, but he didn't argue. If Dame Disapproval thought he was a drunk she might leave him alone.

'Not nearly drunk enough,' he replied, casting around him

with a broad sweep of his hand until he connected with what he was thinking clearly enough to recognise as a woman's breast. It was on the small side but it was firm, encased in lace and fitted his palm perfectly.

Alone and in the dark, Manda had thought things couldn't get any worse until cold fingers had fastened around her arm. That had been the realisation of every childhood nightmare, every creepy movie she had watched from behind half-closed fingers and for a blind second her bogeyman-in-the-dark terror had gone right off the scale.

Then he'd spoken.

The words, admittedly, had not been encouraging, his voice little more than a growl. But the growl had been in English and the knowledge that by some miracle she was not alone, that there was another person in that awful darkness, someone to share the nightmare, dispel the terrible silence, had been so overwhelming that she had almost blubbed with sheer relief.

Thankfully, she had managed to restrain herself, since the overwhelming relief appeared to have been a touch premature.

It was about par for the day that, instead of being incarcerated with a purposeful and valiant knight errant, she had stumbled on some fool who'd been hell-bent on drinking himself to death when the forces of nature had decided to help him out.

'I think you've had quite enough to drink already,' she said a touch acidly.

'Wrong answer. At a time like this there isn't enough alcohol in the world, lady. Unless, of course, you're prepared to divert me with some more interesting alternative?'

And, in case she hadn't got the point, he rubbed a thumb, with shocking intimacy, over her nipple. And then, presumably because she didn't instantly protest, he did it again.

Her lack of protest was not meant as encouragement but,

already prominent from the chill of the underground temple, his touch had reverberated through her body, throwing switches, lighting up dark, long undisturbed places, momentarily robbing her of breath.

By the time she'd gasped in sufficient air to make her feelings felt, they had become confused. In the darkness, the intimacy, heat, beating life force of another body had not felt like an intrusion. Far from it. It had felt like a promise of life.

It was no more than instinct, she told herself; the standard human response in the face of death was to cling to someone, anyone. That thought was enough to bring her back to her senses.

'I don't think so,' she said, belatedly slapping his hand away.

'Please yourself. Let me know if you change your mind.' He rolled away from her and, despite the fact that it was no more than a grope from a drunk, she still missed the human warmth of his touch.

She *wanted* his hand on her breast. Wanted a whole lot more.

Nothing had changed, it seemed. Beneath the hard protective shell she'd built around her, she was as weak and needy as ever.

She'd quickly slipped the buttons on her shirt so that she could lift up the still damp hem to wipe his face. Now she used it to wipe her own throat. Cool her overheated senses.

'It would please me,' she said, 'if you'd give some thought to getting us out of here.'

She snapped out the words, but it was herself she was angry with.

'Why would I do that?' he replied, as she struggled with sore fingers to refasten the small buttons. 'I *like* it here.' Then, 'But I like it here best when I'm alone.'

'In that case I suggest you stay exactly where you are and wait for the next shock to bring the rest of the temple down on top of you. Then you'll be alone until some archaeologist uncovers your bones in another two or three thousand years.'

Jago laughed at the irony of that. A short harsh sound that, even to his own ears, sounded distinctly unpleasant. 'That's an interesting idea, lady, but since I'm not the butler you'll have to see yourself out.' Then, as an afterthought, 'Although if you see that bottle it would be an act of charity…'

'Forget the damn bottle,' she retorted angrily. 'It may have escaped your notice, but you can't see your hand in front of you in here.'

'It's night,' he muttered, finally making an effort to sit up, ignoring the pains shooting through every cramped joint as he explored the floor about him. 'And now I really do need a drink.'

'Only a drunk needs a drink. Is that what you are?'

'Not yet. That takes practice, but give me time…'

He stopped his fruitless search for a bottle of water and stared in the direction of the voice. She was right; it *was* dark. On moonless nights the stars silvered the temple with a faint light and even here, in the lower level, they shone down the shaft cut through the hillside that was aligned so that the full moon, at its highest arc in the sky, lit up the altar.

He blinked, rapidly. It made no difference. And as his mind cleared, it began to dawn on him that something was seriously wrong. The dust. The rubble…

He put his hand to his head in an attempt to still the drummer. 'What day is this?'

'Monday.'

'It's still Monday?'

'I think so. I don't know how long I was out and it's too dark to see my watch, but I don't think it could have been long.'

He propped himself against the nearest wall and tried to remember.

Something about Rob…

'Out?' he asked, leaving the jumble to sort itself out. Definitely not alcohol in Miss Bossy's case. 'What happened to you?'

'Work it out for yourself,' she snapped.

She was halfway to her feet when his hand, sweeping the air in the direction of her voice, connected with her leg and grabbed it. She let out a shriek of alarm.

'Shut up,' he said tightly. 'I've got a headache and I can't think with all that noise.'

'Poor baby,' she crooned with crushing insincerity. Then lashed out with her free leg, her toe connecting with his thigh.

He jerked her other leg from beneath her, which was a mistake since she landed on top of him.

He said one word, but since she'd knocked the breath out of him, only he knew for certain what it was.

Manda considered kicking him again but thought better of it. They needed to stop bickering and start working together and, whoever he was, he had an impressively broad shoulder. The kind built for leaning on.

His shirt, beneath her cheek, had the soft feel that heavy-duty cotton got when it had been worn and washed times without number and the bare skin of his neck smelled of soap.

Maybe he wasn't going to be such a total loss after all…

'Make yourself at home, why don't you,' he said, taking her by the waist and shifting her a little to the right before settling his hands on her backside, at which point she realised that it wasn't only his shoulders that were impressive and…

And what the heck was she thinking?

She rolled off him, biting back a yelp as she landed on what felt like the Rock of Gibraltar. If he knew, he'd laugh.

'Who the hell are you?' she demanded.

'Who the hell are *you*?' he retaliated, definitely not amused. On the contrary, he sounded decidedly irritable. 'And what are you doing here?'

'I asked first.'

There was an ominous silence and it occurred to Manda that, no matter what the provocation, further aggravating a man already in a seriously bad mood was not a particularly bright idea.

It wasn't that she cared what he thought of her, but those broad shoulders of his were going to be an asset since it was obvious that their chances of survival would double if they worked together.

Tricky enough under the best of circumstances.

Team-building was not one of her more developed skills; she tended to work best as top dog. Issuing orders. It worked well with the TV production team she'd put together. Belle, in front of camera, was undoubtedly the star, but she was a professional, used to taking direction.

Daisy… Well, Daisy was learning.

Sensing that on this occasion she was going to need a different approach, she began again by introducing herself.

'Look, we seem to have got off on the wrong foot. My name is Miranda Grenville,' she said, striving, with difficulty, for politeness. 'I'm here taking a short break…'

'In Cordillera? Are you crazy?'

She gritted her teeth, then said, 'Undoubtedly. It has possibilities as a holiday destination, admittedly, but so far none of them have been successfully exploited.'

'Oh, believe me. They've got the exploitation angle covered.'

He didn't sound happy about that, either.

'Not noticeably,' she replied. 'And tourists tend to have a bit of a phobia about earthquakes.'

'In that case they—you—would be well advised to stick to somewhere safer,' he retaliated. 'Try Bournemouth next time.'

'Thank you for your advice. I'll bear it in mind should there ever be a "next time".'

His bad mood was beginning to seriously annoy her, a fact which, if he'd known her, should worry him. That she suspected it wouldn't bother him in the slightest made him interesting. A pain, but interesting…

'Meanwhile, since I'm here—we're here—in the middle of the earthquake that happened while you were sleeping off…' politeness, Manda, politeness '…whatever you were sleeping off, maybe you'd like to help me figure out how we're going to get out of here?'

She spoke in calm, measured tones. Dealing with an idiot had the advantage of making her forget her own fears, it seemed.

He replied briefly in a manner that was neither calm nor measured. Then, having got that off his chest, he said, 'There's been an earthquake?'

'By George he's got it,' she replied sarcastically.

He repeated his first thought, expressing his feelings with a directness that she'd have found difficulty in bettering if she wasn't making a determined effort to play nice. Clearly, this was not the moment to point out that he hadn't completed their introductions.

Whoever he was, he didn't seem to have much time for the social niceties, but the silence went on for a long time and, after a while, she cleared her throat—just to get rid of the dust.

Manda heard him shift in the darkness, felt rather than saw him turn in her direction. 'Tell me,' he said, after what seemed like an age. 'What, in the name of all that's holy, are you doing in a Cordilleran temple in the middle of an earthquake?'

For a moment she considered telling him that it was none

of his damned business. But she needed his help, whoever he was. So she compromised.

'I'll tell you that,' she informed him, 'if you'll tell me what the devil you're doing, drinking yourself to perdition in a Cordilleran temple. At any time.'

Despite the pain in his head, Jago had to admit that this woman had a certain entertainment value and he laughed.

This was not a wise move as his head was swift to remind him. But something about the way she'd come back at him had been so unexpectedly sharp, so refreshingly astringent that he couldn't help himself. And if she was right about the earthquake she got ten out of ten for…something. If only being a pain in the butt.

Admittedly it was a very nicely put together butt…

He began, despite every cell in his body clamouring a warning, to wonder who she was, where she had come from. What she looked like.

Had he, despite his best intentions, started drinking in Rob's bar and been so lost to sense that he'd picked up some lone female tourist looking for a good time and brought her back here with him? If so, he'd signally failed to deliver, he thought, as he searched his memory for a picture to match the voice.

His memory refused to oblige so he was forced to ask, 'Did I pick you up in Rob's bar?'

'Who's Rob?'

'I guess that answers that question…'

'Don't you remember?'

Great butt, smart mouth. Tricky combination. 'If I remembered I wouldn't ask,' he snapped right back, but the scorn in her voice warned him that he was on dangerous ground. And, remembering that kick, it occurred to him that insulting her might not be his best idea.

But where the hell had she come from?

Everything after Rob had thrust that bottle at him was something of a blur, but he hadn't been in the mood to pick up a woman, no matter how warm and willing she was—and actually he was getting very mixed messages about that—but then he'd be the first to admit that he hadn't been thinking too straight.

If only his head didn't hurt so much. He needed to concentrate…

He had a vague memory of driving back up the side of the mountain in a mood as grim as the pagan gods that had guarded the temple and he glared into the darkness as if they had the answer.

It really was dark.

Of his companion he had no more than a vague impression, amplified by that handful of a small, perfectly formed breast. Two handfuls of neat little butt. Tallish, he thought, a bit on the skinny side, but with hair that smelled of childhood innocence…

He stopped the thought right there.

Women were born devious and he was done with the whole treacherous, self-serving sex.

He'd driven back from the coast on his own, he was certain of that, but if he hadn't picked her up, where the devil had she come from?

He scrubbed at his face with his hands in an effort to clear away the confusion. Then, dragging his fingers through his hair, he winced as he encountered a damn great lump and a stickiness that couldn't be anything but blood.

It seemed that the throbbing ache in his head was the result of a collision with something hard rather than the effects of Cordilleran brandy. Unless he had fallen out of the camp-bed he'd set up down here after the rest of the team had left when the rains set in. Going home to their families.

It was drier than his hut in the village during the rains. Quieter. And, without Fliss to distract him, he'd got a lot of work done.

He blinked. The lack of light was beginning to irritate him. He wanted to be able to see this woman. Was she another student backpacking her way around the globe? If so, she'd chosen the wrong day to drop in looking for work experience…

'Okay, I didn't pick you up in a bar,' he began, then stopped. That was too loud. Much too loud. 'So where—?'

'You didn't pick me up anywhere.' Her disembodied voice enunciated each word slowly and carefully, as if speaking to someone for whom English was a foreign language. 'I'm fussy about who I hang around with.'

'Really? My mistake,' he said, heavy on the irony. 'So how did you get here?'

'By bus.'

Jago laughed again and this time he was genuinely amused at the thought of this hoity-toity madam flagging down one of the island's overcrowded buses and piling in with the goats and chickens.

Apparently she didn't share his sense of humour.

'What's so funny?'

'Not a thing,' he said, meaning it. Then, 'What did you say your name was? Amanda…?' The effort of remembering her surname was too much and he let it go.

'Miranda,' she corrected. 'My friends call me Manda but, since I have no plans for a long acquaintance with you, whoever you are, we might as well keep it formal.'

'Suits me,' he replied with feeling. Then, 'I'm Jago,' he said, begrudgingly giving up his name at the same time as he remembered hers. Grenville. That was what she had said. The name was vaguely familiar, but he didn't recognise her voice. Maybe the face… He could strike a match, he supposed, but really it was too much effort and, despite his desire to see her, he wasn't ready for anything that bright. 'No,' he said. 'Sorry. I give up. I've forgotten where we met.'

'It sounds to me as if you gave up a long time ago but I'll put you out of your misery. We've never met.'

'I may be careless, lady—'

'Will you please stop calling me that,' she interrupted crossly. 'My name is Miranda—'

'I may be careless about some things, *Miranda*,' he said, with heavy emphasis on her name, 'but I've given up on inviting strangers home to tea.'

'Why is that, I wonder? Are you frightened they might steal the silver?'

He wished, but confined his response to, 'Who are you? What are you?'

CHAPTER FOUR

GOOD question, Manda thought. One to which the people she lived and worked with could give any number of answers, most of them wrong.

'Does it matter? I promise I won't run off with the spoons,' she said, pulling a face, confident that he would not see it.

It was a long time since afternoon tea had been part of his social life if she was any judge of the situation. But although a little verbal fencing in the dark with an unknown, unseen man might have been amusing at any other time, she'd had enough. She'd had enough of the dark, enough of being scared, enough of him.

'Oh, forget it. Just point me in the direction of the nearest exit and I'll be only too happy to leave you alone.'

Jago was beyond such politeness. His head was pounding like the percussion section of the London Philharmonic and all he wanted to do was lie down and close his eyes. 'You got yourself in here. Reverse the process,' he advised. 'You'll be home in no time.' Then added, 'Don't forget to shut the door on your way out.'

An explosive little sound echoed around the dark chamber. 'Sober up and look around you, Mr Jago. There aren't any doors.'

He groaned.

Why was it, with the whole world of wonderful things to choose from, God had picked women as the opposite sex?

'Time and white ants have done their worst,' he admitted, 'but I was speaking metaphorically. Entrance. Opening. Ingress. Access. Take your pick.'

'What on earth is the matter with you? Did a lump of stone fall on your head? Or have you drunk yourself quite senseless?'

'That was the plan,' he said, hoping that she might finally take the hint, shut up and leave him in peace. 'It doesn't seem to have worked. How did you get in here, anyway? This area is restricted.'

'To whom?'

To whom? He rubbed his hand over his face again—carefully avoiding the lump on his hairline this time—in an attempt to bring it back to life. Whoever this female was, she couldn't be a student. No student he'd ever met could be bothered to speak English with that precision. He eased himself into a sitting position. 'To me, Miranda Grenville. To me. And you weren't invited.'

'I wouldn't have come if I had been,' she declared. 'This is the last place I want to be, but I'm afraid you'll have to stand in line to send your complaint to a higher authority.'

'Oh? And which higher authority would that be?' he enquired, knowing full well that it was a mistake, that he would regret it, but completely unable to help himself. There was something about this woman that just got under his skin.

'Mother Nature?' she offered. 'I was simply standing on a footpath, quietly minding my own business, when the ground opened up beneath me and I fell through your roof. As I believe I've already mentioned, while you were busy drowning your sorrows there was an earthquake.'

'An earthquake?' He frowned. Wished he hadn't. 'A genuine, honest-to-God earthquake?'

'It seemed very real to me.'

'Not just a tremor?'

'Not a tremor. I was in Brazil last year when there was a tremor,' she explained. 'I promise you this was the real deal.'

Jago fumbled in his pocket for a box of matches. As he struck one, it flared briefly, for a moment blinding him with the sudden brightness so near to his face, but as his eyes adjusted to the light, he stared around, momentarily speechless at the destruction that surrounded him.

The outside walls of the temple, with their stone carvings, had been pushed inward and the floor that he had spent months digging down through the debris of centuries to clear was now little more than rubble.

The woman was right. It would have taken a serious earthquake to have caused this much damage.

It had, all in all, been one hell of a day.

A small anguished sound caught his attention and he turned to his unwelcome companion, temporarily forgotten as he had surveyed the heartbreaking destruction of the centuries-old temple complex built by a society whose lives he had devoted so much time to understanding. Reconstructing.

He swore and dropped the match as it burned down to his fingers.

The darkness after the brief flare of light seemed, if anything, more intense, thicker, substantial enough to cut into slices and in a moment of panic he groped in the box for another match.

It was empty.

There was a new carton somewhere, but his supplies were stored at the far end of the temple. And the far end of the temple, as he'd just seen, was no more…

'We're trapped, aren't we?'

Her voice had, in that instant of light, lost all that assured bravado.

'Of course we're not trapped,' he snapped back. The last thing he needed was hysterics. 'I just need a minute to figure the best way out.'

'There isn't one. I saw—'

Too late. Her voice was rising in panic and his own clammy moment of fear was still too close to risk her going over the edge and taking him with her.

'Shut up and let me think.'

She gave a juddering little hiccup as she struggled to obey him, to control herself, but he forced himself to ignore the instinct to reach out, hold her, comfort her.

She'd said she'd been standing on the path, presumably the one leading to the acropolis, but she couldn't have been alone.

'How did you get up here?' His voice was sharper this time, demanding an answer.

'I told you,' she said. 'By bus.'

His head still hurt like hell, but the realisation that he was caught up in the aftermath of an earthquake had done much to concentrate his mind. He'd broken the seal on the bottle of brandy, but the minute the liquor had touched his lips he'd set it down, recognising the stupidity of drinking himself into oblivion.

That was what Rob had done when his yacht had gone down in a storm. Was still doing. Washed up on the beach and pretty much a wreck himself...

'What kind of bus?' he demanded. 'Nobody lives up here.' The locals avoided the area, ancient folk memory keeping them well away from the place.

'Not a local bus. I was on a sightseeing trip.'

He grunted.

A sightseeing trip. Of course.

The government was trying attract tourism investment, but Cordillera would be hard pushed to compete with the other established resorts of the Far East unless there was something else, something different to tempt the jaded traveller.

The ruins of a sexed-up ancient civilisation would do as well as anything. And once the finance was fixed, the resorts built, the visitors would flood in.

He hadn't wanted hordes of tourists trampling about the place disturbing his work. As archaeological director of the site he had the authority to keep them out and he'd used it.

He'd seen the damage that could be done, knew that once there was a market for artefacts, it wouldn't be long before the locals would forget their fear and start digging up the forest for stuff, chiselling chunks of their history to sell to tourists.

He'd known that sooner or later he would be overruled, but in the meantime he'd kept everything but the bare bones of his discoveries to himself, delaying publication for as long as possible.

Impatient for results he could exploit to his advantage, it seemed that Felipe Dominez had looked for another way.

'I hadn't realised that we were already on the tourist route,' he said bitterly.

'I don't think you are,' she assured him. 'If a trade delegation whose flight was delayed hadn't been shanghaied into taking the trip, it would have been me, a couple of dozen other unfortunates who believed that Cordillera was going to be the next big thing and the driver-cum-tour-guide. Why the business people bothered I can't imagine.'

'I can,' he said sourly, 'if the alternative was the doubtful comforts of the airport departure lounge.'

'Maybe, but at least there they'd be sure someone was going to try and dig them out of the rubble. Here—'

He didn't think it wise to let her dwell on what was likely to be her fate 'here'.

'What happened to the rest of your party?' he cut in quickly.

'It was hot and sticky and I was suffering from a severe case of ancient culture fatigue so I decided to sit out the second half of the tour. When the ground opened up and swallowed me I was on my own.'

'But you'll be missed?'

'Will I?' Manda asked.

In the panic she knew it was unlikely. Even supposing anyone else had survived. They could easily have suffered the same fate as she had and she was unbelievably lucky not to have been buried beneath tons of debris… Maybe. That would at least have been quick.

Trapped down here, the alternative might prove to be a lot worse, she thought, and dug what was left of her nails into the palms of her hands.

Breathe…

'I suppose that eventually someone will wonder what happened to me,' she admitted. 'Right now, I suspect they'll all be too busy surviving, Mr Jago, so if you could put your mind to the problem of how we're going to get out of here I really would be grateful.' There was a long pause. 'Please.'

That belated 'please' bothered Jago.

His uninvited guest had not, so far, displayed any real inclination to politeness. On the contrary, she'd been full of spit and fire, swiftly recovering from that momentary wobble a few moments ago.

'Miranda?'

'Yes?'

About to suggest that under the circumstances they could probably both do with a drink, he changed his mind. In the unlikely event that he managed to find the bottle of brandy in one piece, it might be wiser to hang on to it. Maybe later she would be grateful for the possibility of at least temporary oblivion. Maybe they both would.

Instead he said, 'Most people just call me Jago.'

There was a small silence. 'And what does everyone else call you?' she asked, still fighting a rearguard action against the fear, keeping the edge going.

Soft, sweet words, he thought. All of them lies. 'Nothing fit for the ears of a lady.' Then, eager to change the subject, 'Were you hurt when you fell?'

'Just a few bruises,' she said, with a carelessness that suggested she was being economical with the truth. 'What about you?'

'Not bad, apart from a pain in my leg where someone kicked me.' Keeping it sharp was good. She was keeping up a great front so far; kindness might just have her in pieces, which was something he could do without. 'And a headache which probably has more to do with the large lump on my forehead and less to do with alcohol than I originally supposed. But I'll probably live.'

'If we get out of here.'

'We'll get out. I just need to get my bearings.'

'Maybe you should light another match.'

'I would,' he replied. Then, since there was no way to save her from reality, 'Unfortunately that was the last one.'

'What?'

It took a moment for the disaster to sink in. Despite the devastation revealed in those few moments as the match flame had burned away the darkness, the very promise of light had driven back a little of Manda's fear. But no more matches meant no more light and all at once the blackness, thick enough to touch, seemed to be pressing against her face, smothering her.

She scrambled to her feet, brushing frantically at her face with her hands as if somehow she could rid herself of it, rid herself of the sense of being suffocated.

'Don't stand up!'

Jago's urgent warning came too late and, stumbling on the uneven, broken floor, she saved herself by grasping a handful of cloth as she fell against him.

He grunted as she went down, collapsing against him, taking him down with her. He flung his arms about her in an attempt to stop her from hurting herself further, but in her panic she began to fight him, threshing about to free herself.

'Steady now,' Jago muttered into her hair as he hung on, recognising the mindless fear that had overtaken her. 'Calm down, for pity's sake. You'll only hurt yourself.'

And him. He didn't bother to mention that just in case it gave her ideas.

It made no difference since she didn't seem to hear him, but continued to struggle fiercely like a trapped animal and he winced and swore as she broke free, her elbow catching him a glancing blow on the jaw.

'We'll be all right,' he said, keeping his voice low, doing his best to reassure her. 'I'll get us out of here.'

She wasn't listening. Beyond simple reason, she was fighting blindly to escape and, swearing as he took another blow, he pressed his face into her breast to protect himself as he struggled to hold her.

'Let me go!' she demanded. 'I don't need you to get me out of here. Stick with your bottle…' And she continued to kick and writhe until she connected solidly with his shin.

It was enough. The girl was slender but she had a kick like a mule and he rolled over, pinning her to the ground.

'Be still,' he warned, abandoning reassurance, making it an order. She continued to heave and buck beneath him, uncaring of the dust rising in choking clouds around them, too lost in her own spiralling hysteria to hear him, or to obey him even if she could.

He'd have to let go to slap her and while the temptation was almost overwhelming—he was still feeling that kick—he chose the only other alternative left open to him and kissed her.

It was brutal but effective, cutting off the stream of invective, cutting off her breath and, taken by surprise, she went rigid beneath him. And then, just as swiftly, she was clinging to him, her mouth hot and eager as she pressed against him, desperate for the warmth of a human body. For comfort in the darkness. A no-holds-barred kiss without a hidden agenda. Pure, honest, raw need that tapped into something deep inside him. And for a seemingly endless moment he answered it without question.

As suddenly as it began it was over. Miranda slumped back against the cracked and—now—sloping floor of the temple. Jago, his body flattening her to the ground, was horribly aware of the huge shuddering sob that swept through her.

'I'm sorry,' she said and for a hideous moment he thought she was apologising for kissing him. 'I thought I had it.' She shivered again. 'I thought I had it under control…'

'Hey, come on. You're doing fine,' he said, lifting his hand to her face in a gesture that was meant to offer comfort, reassurance but she flinched away from him.

'Don't! Don't ever do that again!'

'I could just as easily have slapped you,' he said.

'I wish you had.'

'Fine. I'll remember you said that the next time you get hysterical.'

'In your dreams, Mr Jago,' she declared fervently.

'In yours, Ms Grenville.'

In truth they were both breathing rather more heavily and her verbal rejection was certainly not being followed up by her body. Or his. Being this close to a stranger, to a woman who was no more than curves that fitted his body like a glove, soft skin, a scent in the darkness, was doing something to his head.

Her hair, a short, sleek bob, was like silk beneath his hand and she smelled so sweet and fresh after the damp, cloying air of the jungle; a primrose after the heavy, drugging scent of the huge trumpet lilies that hung from the trees, drenching the air of the forest.

She was slender but strong, with a firm leggy body that he guessed would be perfectly at home on horseback. He knew the type. Had grown up with girls who sounded—and felt—like this. Haughty girls who knew their worth, girls bred for men who had titles, or with bank balances large enough to cancel out the lack of one. Made for swish hotels and six hundred-thread Egyptian cotton sheets rather than a stone floor and a man who'd walked away from such luxuries, from everything that went with it, a long time ago.

He knew—they both did—that if he kissed her again, it would be slow and hot and she'd be with him every step of the way and the thought of taking a woman like her on the cold stone, amidst the rubble, without any pretence, any of the ritual dance that a man was expected to go through before he could claim such a prize, was a temptation almost beyond measure.

'Jago?' Her voice, soft and low, pulled him away from his dark thoughts and he finally moved, putting an inch between them, knowing that it was his damaged ego, pride rather than

passion, that was driving his libido. Demanding satisfaction.
'Who are you?'

He'd asked her the same question. Her reply had been to
ask whether it mattered.

Did it?

He'd grown up knowing exactly who he was, what his
future held. He'd walked away from all of it, built another life.
Now he was just a fool who had allowed a girl with a hot body
to take him to the cleaners.

A fool who was about to become a serious embarrassment
to a Cordilleran government minister who he suspected might
find it very convenient if he never emerged from the ruins of
his own excavations.

'Me?' he said. 'I told you. I'm the man who's going to get
us out of here.'

'Right.'

'You don't sound convinced.'

Oh, she was convinced, Manda thought. If it was possible,
he would do it.

She'd briefly glimpsed Jago's silhouette in the flare of the
match; a dark mop of hair, a strong neck, broad shoulders that,
as the light had gone out, had remained a ghostly negative
imprint in the darkness.

The impression had been of power: not the weakness of a
man who'd surrendered to the easy oblivion of drink. His
face had been taut, firm to the touch. Beneath her fingers, his
body had the sinewy, muscled strength of a man who knew
how to work. And his mouth—she felt the weakness return;
his mouth had not tasted of stale alcohol, but had the clean,
hard, demanding authority of a man who was confident of his
power to overwhelm all and any objections.

But what woman would object?

Despite their bad start, every instinct told her that he was the real deal, a true alpha male, and she'd come within a heartbeat of succumbing to an intimacy that she'd denied herself for so long, aware that, if only for a little while, this man had the ability to wipe out the darkness.

She had resisted the temptation, knowing that when the darkness returned it would be even worse.

Realising that she was still pressing herself against him, clinging close for support, warmth, comfort—something darker and more compelling—she pulled away and he didn't make any move to stop her.

'Convinced?' she said, using the words, a disparaging tone to her voice, to put more distance between them, distract herself from the throbbing of lips that hadn't been kissed that way in a very long time. Actually, had never been kissed that way. No gentleman ever kissed a woman like that. More was the pity… 'Oh, please! I can tell when it's the drink talking.'

'Really?' There was a long pause and in the darkness Manda fancied he was smiling, if a touch grimly, not fooled for a minute. 'Well, maybe you're right, but since I'm the only help you're going to get, you might be wise to brush up your manners, Miranda Grenville.'

'Why?' She just couldn't stop herself… 'Will they help us burrow our way out of here?'

'No. But it might make the time spent doing it a touch less disagreeable.'

Manda cleared her throat of dust. She knew she wasn't behaving at all well, but then behaving badly had been her default mode for a very long time. She really would have to try and do better now that she was a godmother, even one whose avowed aim was to lead her little charges astray.

As if…

Unless spoiling them rotten came under that heading. Not just with toys, sparklies, outings and treats. She was going to *really* spoil them with words, hugs, being there for them when they needed a hand in the dark, by giving herself. She was going to love them, cherish them. And make sure they knew it.

Given a chance.

She sucked in her breath as she faced the very real possibility that she might never see them again. The knowledge that if she didn't she would have no one to blame but herself. She'd been weak, running away, unable to face up to the demons that haunted her.

Who was she to judge a man like Jago?

If she had to spend much time in this ghastly place, she would probably be driven to blur reality by whatever means came to hand. Or leave.

But maybe he couldn't do that.

He was after all working here…

'O-okay,' she managed. 'Pax?' He responded with a grunt. Obviously she was going to have to work harder on her social skills. 'So, macho man, what's the plan?'

'Give me a minute.' Then, 'I don't suppose you have painkillers about your person by any chance?'

'In my bag,' she said. 'Wherever that is. Until we get some light you'll just have to suffer.'

No. Even *in extremis* she just couldn't bring herself to play nice…

'That's a pity. I don't think too well with a headache.'

'That must be extremely limiting.' Then, as he began to move, 'Where are you going?'

'Not far,' he assured her dryly at the sudden rise in her voice. 'My supplies were stored at the far end of the temple. I want to see if I can find anything useful.'

'Another bottle of cheap brandy?'

'This isn't the Ritz, lady. You'll have to take what you can get.'

'Mine's water, since you're offering.'

The drink thing was getting old, Jago thought. Okay, she was scared—she had every right to be; he wasn't overcome with an urge to burst into song himself—but a woman with a smart mouth wasn't about to provoke much in the way of sympathy. Even if it was a mouth that had promised heaven on earth.

'If I find any, I'll save you a mouthful,' he said, making a move.

'No! Hold on, I'm coming with you,' she said, grabbing a handful of shirt, and the sudden note of desperation in her voice got to him.

'There's no need, really,' he said. Disengaging her hand from his shirt front and putting his mouth to her ear, he whispered, 'I promise if I find some I'll share. Scout's honour.'

Furious, she backed off. 'You've never been a scout. Anyone less "prepared"…'

'Tell me, are you always this disagreeable?' he enquired.

'Only when I've been trapped underground by an earthquake.' He didn't answer. 'Okay. I have a low tolerance of incompetence,' she admitted. 'Not that I'm saying you're incompetent. I'm sure you're very good at…'

'Getting drunk?'

She gave a little shivery sigh. 'N-no. You're no more drunk than I am.'

'No,' he said, 'although I'll admit that I did consider drowning my sorrows if it'll make you happy. Fortunately for both of us, I thought better of it but it's likely the bottle broke when the earthquake hit so be careful where you put your hands and knees. And don't grab at me, okay? I'm not going anywhere without you.'

'No,' she said again. Then, 'I'm…sorry.'

Anything that difficult to say had to be sincere and by way of reply he wrapped his fingers about her wrist.

It was slender and he could feel the delicate bones beneath her skin, the rapid beat of her pulse. It was a wonder that something so fragile could have survived un-damaged as she had fallen through the roof. She had been lucky. So far.

'Yes, well, maybe we could both do better. Now, let's see if we can find a light.' As she made a move to stand up, he held her down. 'On your knees, Miranda. Breaking an ankle down here isn't going to improve matters.'

'Know-all,' she muttered.

'You know, maybe you should try not talking for a while,' he suggested.

'You should be so lucky,' she replied, grinning despite everything. Riling this man might be the last fun she ever had so she might as well enjoy it. 'So, have you any idea where you are?'

'I know where this was yesterday,' he replied, bringing her back to earth with a bump. 'Once we reach one of the walls I'll have a better idea of the situation.'

Keeping his free hand extended in front of him, Jago swept the air at head height; it would be stupid to knock himself out on a block of stone. Easy, but stupid and he'd used up his quota of stupid for this lifetime.

Despite the blackness, he sensed the wall a split second before he came into contact with it and, placing his hand flat against the surface, he began to feel for the carvings that would tell him where he was.

'I'll need both hands for this,' he said, but rather than aban-doning her while he searched for something that would tell him where he was, he turned and pressed her fingers against his belt. 'Just hang on to that for a moment.'

Manda didn't argue. His belt was made from soft, well worn leather and she hooked her fingers under it so that her knuckles were tucked up against his waist as he moved slowly forward, her face close enough to his back to feel the warmth emanating from his body.

'Well?' she demanded after what seemed like an endless silence. He didn't answer and that was even more frightening than his silence. 'Jago!'

'I think I've found the eagle,' he said.

'The eagle?' Manda remembered the unfinished carving on the stone beside the path.

'It had a special place in the life of the people who lived here, watching over them.'

'In return for the entrails of young virgins?' she asked, trying to recall the stuff she'd heard in the television interview of the well-endowed archaeologist.

'You read the *Courier*?' He didn't bother to disguise his disgust.

'Not unless I'm desperate. Should I?'

'Someone wrote a book about this place and the *Courier* ran excerpts from it. It was pitched at the sensational end of the market.'

'They wouldn't be interested otherwise. And no, I didn't read it, but I did catch a few minutes of the author when she was doing the rounds of the television chat shows a few weeks back. Very striking. For an archaeologist.'

'Yes.'

'I take it you know her?' Then, when he didn't answer, 'Who is she?'

'No one who need worry about becoming a virgin sacrifice,' he replied and there was no disguising the edge in his voice. He was, it seemed, speaking from experience. Was she the reason he'd been thinking about taking to the bottle? She didn't ask. She didn't want to know and, rapidly changing the subject, she prompted, 'Tell me about the eagle. The one that you've found.'

He turned away from her, looking up. 'It used to be above the altar stone.'

'So?'

'In the ceiling above the altar stone.'

Earlier that day Jago had been certain that life didn't hold much meaning for him. The sudden realisation of how close he had come to losing it put a whole new slant on the situation.

'Okay, let's try this way,' he said, moving to the left too quickly, catching Miranda off balance and she let out a yelp of pain.

'What is it?' Jago demanded impatiently.

'Nothing. I jabbed my hand on something, that's all—'

'Glass?' Jago reached back, took the hand she was cradling to her breast and ran his thumb over her palm and fingers to check for blood. If the bottle had broken, if she'd cut herself… But her hand was dry. 'It must have been a piece of stone. Be careful, okay?'

She just laughed, deriding him for a fool and who could blame her?

'I mean it!' he said angrily, knowing full well that what had happened had been his fault. 'I'm sorry.'

'It's okay. I understand. It's worse than you thought, isn't it?'

'It's not great,' he admitted.

'So? Are we going to get out?'

She spoke directly, her voice demanding an honest answer from him, but Jago had spent a lot of time working alone in the Cordilleran temples and his hearing had grown acute in the silence. He heard the underlying tremor, the fear she was taking such pains to hide.

CHAPTER FIVE

'WE'LL get out. I'm not promising you that it will be quick, or easy.' Jago knew there was little point in putting an optimistic gloss on it. She had seen the devastation for herself in the flare of the match. 'Even if, in the confusion, your tour party don't immediately miss you, I have no doubt that your family are already making things hot for officials at the Foreign Office.'

Her response was a tiny shivering sigh. 'I'm afraid if you're relying on that to get us out of here, we really are in trouble. I…I'm sort of taking time out from my family. They have no idea where I am.'

'Are you telling me that you didn't even send your mother a postcard?' he asked, tutting.

'I don't have a mother, but even if I had…' She broke off. 'I mean— Wish you were here? Would you?'

'Point taken,' he said, his pitiful attempt at levity falling flat. He should have known better. He hadn't just taken time out from his family, he'd walked out of their lives fifteen years ago and never looked back. 'Not to worry. If no one misses you, there are plenty of people who know I'm out here.'

He hoped that would hold her for the moment. That she wouldn't realise that if the whole island had been hit as hard as this there wouldn't be anyone with the time or the energy to care what had happened to him, to any of them. Not until it was too late, anyway.

He continued to hold her hand. Her skin, beneath his own callused palms, was soft. Her fingers long and ringless. Then, as his thumb brushed over the pads of her fingers, he realised that they had taken a pounding. They were rough, the skin torn, her nails broken where she'd clawed at the ground as she'd fallen.

She must have been hurt, he realised, but she wasn't complaining.

'Come on,' he said, with a briskness he was far from feeling. 'This won't buy the baby a new bonnet.'

And this time when she laughed it was with wry amusement. 'When was the last time you bought a baby a bonnet, Jago?'

'Now that, Miss Grenville, would be telling.'

'Manda.'

'Excuse me? You've decided that I'm a friend?'

'I've decided that I don't like being called "lady" or Miss Grenville and I never liked Miranda.'

'Why not?'

'It doesn't matter. Please yourself. Shall we get on?'

There was a long pause, then he released her hand. 'I'm moving to the left.'

She shuffled after him, studiously ignoring a stream of muttered oaths as the floor shook beneath them once more. He turned and caught her before she went down this time, holding her against him, tucking her safe against his shoulder. With her face pressed into his chest, his body protecting her from falling debris, Manda felt ridiculously secure, despite the fact that some vast megalith could at any moment crush the pair of them.

'We really must stop meeting like this,' Jago murmured when everything was quiet, continuing to hold her, her face buried in the hollow of his shoulder, her cheek tight against the heavy cotton of his shirt. The beat of his heart a solid base counterpoint to her own rapid pulse rate and in the darkness she clung to him as if to a lover.

She should move but, afraid of more aftershocks, her courage failed her and she couldn't make herself pull away.

It was Jago who moved first. 'Keep your eyes closed,' he said, shaking off the grit and rubble that had fallen on him.

'Okay, now?'

'No. Wait…' He rubbed his hands clean against his shirt then, very gently, laid them over her face, brushing away the dust from her lids and lashes.

'Okay?' he asked.

'Okay,' she said, close to tears as she slid her hands into his hair, a thick mop of unruly curls, using her fingers to comb out the small pieces of stone. Sweeping her fingertips across a wide forehead, pausing at an impressive bump.

It was little wonder he had a headache, she thought, wishing she hadn't been quite so horrible about that, and on an impulse she kneeled up to kiss it better, before sweeping the pads of her fingers over dusty eyelids, bony cheeks, down the length of a firm jaw. Feeling the stubble of a day-old beard. Discovering the landscape of his face, imprinting its contours in her memory.

He grasped her wrist as she rubbed her thumb across his mouth, stopping her, and for a moment they remained locked together, the pad of her thumb against his lower lip. Then, without a word, he dropped her hand, looped his arm about her waist and turned away, moving slowly along the face of the wall, apparently exploring the carvings with the tips of his fingers as he continued to try and make sense of their surroundings.

'My stuff should be along here,' he said after a while.

'Well, let's get to it,' she said, feeling as if she'd been holding her breath since that moment when anything might have happened. She made a move forward but he didn't let go, stopping her. 'What are we waiting for?' she asked scratchily. 'Your pack of matches won't crawl out all by itself and jump into your hand.'

'True, but blundering off into the dark isn't going to help and if we're not careful we could bring the whole lot down on us.'

'True. And if we stay here talking about it long enough another aftershock might just save us the job,' she replied impatiently. His closeness had become too intimate and she tried to tug free. His grip tightened just enough to warn her to keep still.

'Slow down,' he said, his arm around her waist immovable, powerful. Controlling. Their brief moment of rapport now history.

'Why?' she demanded. 'Despite your little pep talk back there, I do realise that no one is likely to be looking for us any time soon.'

'Do you? Really?'

'What's to understand?'

She'd been in the wrong place at the wrong time. Only time would tell whether she had been lucky or unlucky, but one thing was sure, she wasn't going to sit around and wait for someone to come and dig them out.

'I've seen these things on television, Jago. I know that out there it'll be total chaos and, until we get any indication to the contrary, we have to assume we're on our own. The longer we sit around doing nothing, the weaker we'll get.' Then, with a surge of excitement. 'No, wait!'

'What?'

'In my bag! I've got a cellphone…'

'Miranda—'

'If it survived the fall.'

'And if we could get a signal up here,' he replied heavily, brutally crushing the wild surge of hope.

'There's no signal?'

She felt, rather than saw him shake his head, heard the muttered oath as, too late, he recalled the blow he'd sustained.

'Are you okay?' The chances were that he was suffering from concussion at the very least.

'I'll live,' he replied. 'Is there anything else that might be useful in this bag of yours?'

She suspected he'd asked more to keep her from falling apart again than for any other reason. She wasn't fooled into thinking that it was personal, that he'd felt anything beyond lust when he'd kissed her. She mustn't make that mistake ever again.

He'd protected her from falling masonry because, injured, she'd be even more of a liability. Even a speck of dust in her eye could have caused problems and he needed her fit and strong, not a feeble hysteric.

Heaven forbid he should feel obliged to kiss her again.

Heaven help him if he slapped her.

'Water,' she said. 'I've got a bottle of water.' She thought about it. 'Make that half a bottle of water.' Right now she would have given anything to have a mouthful of that. 'Some mints. Pens. Wipes.' She could really use one of those right now, too. What else? Her journal—no, forget that. 'A foot spray—'

'A *foot spray*?'

'To cool your feet. When you've been walking in hot weather.'

'Right. So, apart from the water and mints, that would be a "no" then,' he said, definitely underwhelmed.

Just as well she hadn't mentioned the deodorant and waterless antiseptic hand wash.

'No matches, torch, string?'

'String?' She very nearly laughed out loud. 'We're talking about a designer bag here. An object of desire for which, I'll have you know, there is a year-long waiting list. Not the pocket of some grubby little boy.'

'So you're the kind of woman who spends telephone numbers on a handbag. I hope I'm not meant to be impressed.'

'It's a matter of supreme indifference to me—'

'I'm glad to hear it,' he said, cutting her off. 'I'm far more interested in its contents.'

And he was right, damn him…

'I've got one of those little travel sewing kits,' she offered sarcastically. 'It has some cotton in it, if you're looking for an Ariadne solution to finding your way out of this maze of ruins.' Then, 'Ruined ruins…'

'A pick and shovel would be more useful, but I accept that's too much to expect. I'll bear the offer of needle and thread in mind, though, in case I'm driven to the point where sewing your mouth shut seems like a good idea.'

'There are safety pins in the kit for that, always assuming I don't use them on you first.'

'Well, now we've got all that out of the way, is there anything that might be in the slightest bit of use to us, because I'm not wasting time hunting for it in the unlikely event that my feet get hot.'

'Wait! There's a mini-light on my keyring,' she replied, as she continued to mentally sift through the contents of her bag. 'It came out of a Christmas cracker, but it's better than nothing.'

'A Christmas cracker?'

'You have a problem with Christmas crackers?' she demanded.

Last year had been her first ever proper family Christmas. Tinsel, a tree covered with bright ornaments, silly presents stacked beneath it. It had been Daisy's idea of a good time, but they'd all been seduced by the complete lack of sophistication, the simple joy of a big fat turkey with all the trimmings, the bright red and green crackers for them to pull, the paper hats, silly jokes and plastic gifts.

Her cracker had contained a tiny light for illuminating locks that she'd hung on her silver Tiffany keyring.

'There's an attack alarm, too,' she offered.

'Did that come out of a cracker, too?'

'No. That wouldn't be very festive, would it?' Then, 'What about you? I saw some tools in one of the temples when we passed the entrance earlier. Was that this temple?'

'The upper chamber, yes.'

'Upper?' Then they were underground? She didn't ask. She really didn't want to think about that. 'The guide said it was too dangerous to enter.'

'He was right. I tend to get seriously bad-tempered when heavy-footed tourists tramp all over my work.'

'Oh. I assumed it was something to do with engineering works.'

'Engineering?'

'Making the place safe for people dumb enough to think this was a good way to spend an afternoon?' Then, when he didn't bother to answer, 'Obviously not. So—what? You're an archaeologist?'

'Not *an* archaeologist. *The* archaeologist. The archaeological director of this site, to be precise.'

'Oh…' She frowned. All feminist ideals aside, she had to admit that it sounded rather more likely than that female in the clinging frock raising a sweat wielding a shovel. 'So who was the woman on the television chat show?'

She felt him stiffen. 'An opportunist with an agenda,' he said tightly. Then, 'I'm sorry. An engineer would undoubtedly be a lot more use to you right now.'

'I don't know about that.' Those sinewy arms were clearly used to hard physical work. 'At least you know your way around, although, since I'm a heavy-footed tourist, maybe I'd better go and hunt for my attack alarm.'

'Please yourself, but if you think setting it off will bring someone rushing to your rescue—'

'No.' And, pressed hard up against him, deprived of sight but with all her other senses working overtime, she said, 'I seem to be in rather more trouble than I thought.'

'You have no idea,' he murmured, his mouth so close to her ear that the stubble on his chin grated against her neck and she could feel his breath against her cheek.

She remembered the feel of his lip against her thumb and it was a struggle to keep from swallowing nervously.

Nerves might be a justifiable reaction under the circumstances, but he'd know it was prompted by her nearness to him, rather than the situation they were in, and that would never do.

Instead, she turned her head so that she was face to face with him in the dark, so close that she could feel the heat of his skin and, lowering her voice to little more than a whisper, she said, 'Do we have time for this, Jago?'

In the intensity of the silence, she could have sworn she heard the creak of muscle as his face creased into a grin. A grin that she could hear in his voice as he said, 'Tough little thing, aren't you?'

And, in spite of everything, she was grinning herself as she said, 'You have no idea.'

For a moment they knelt in that close circle with every sense intensified by the darkness, aware of each other in ways that only those deprived of sight could ever be.

The slight rise and fall of Jago's chest, the slow, steady thud of his heartbeat through her palm.

She could almost taste the pulsing heat of his body.

There was an intimacy, an awareness between them that, under different circumstances, would have had them ripping each other's clothes off.

Or maybe these were exactly the circumstances…

'Okay,' Jago said abruptly, leaning back, putting a little distance between them. 'We need your light, no matter how small it is, and the water. I want you to quarter the floor. Keep low, hands flat on the floor to steady you in case there's another shock. Watch out for broken glass.'

'Yes, sir!' If her knees weren't so sore, she'd have snapped them to attention. 'What are you going to be doing in the meantime?'

'Putting my feet up and waiting for you to get on with it?' he offered, since they were back to sarcasm city. No doubt it was a lot safer than the alternative. 'Or maybe I'll be trying to find a way out. There must be an opening somewhere.'

'Wouldn't we be able to see it if there was?' she asked, in no hurry to let go of her only contact with humanity. To be alone in the darkness.

Or was it letting go of Jago that was the problem? Maddening and gentle, dictatorial and tender by turns, she was becoming perilously attached to the man.

'This chamber is at a lower level so it may not be obvious,

especially if it's dark outside. The chances are that we're going to be climbing out, so you'd better be wearing sensible shoes.'

'Perish the thought.'

'I hope you're kidding…'

Of course she was kidding! As if anyone with an atom of sense would go walkabout wearing open-toed sandals in a tropical forest that was undoubtedly infested with all manner of creepy-crawlies.

'Leave me to worry about my feet,' she replied. 'Just get us out of here.'

'Trust me.'

'Trust? Trust a man?' And, suddenly aware of the ridiculous way she was clinging to his hand, she let go. She did not cling… 'Now you're really in cloud-cuckoo-land.'

'Believe me, if I was in the mood to laugh, I'd be in hysterics at the irony of being forced to rely on a woman,' he assured her without the slightest trace of humour, 'but in the meantime I suggest we both take a trip with the cuckoos and pool our resources until we get out of here.'

And, as if to make his point, he found her arm, sliding his down it until he reached her own hand, picking it up and wrapping his fingers around it. Reconnecting with her in the darkness.

An unexpected wave of relief swept over her and it was all she could do to stop herself from tightening her grip, holding him close.

'What do you say, Miranda? Shall we suspend hostilities, save the battle of the sexes for the duration?'

She wanted to ask why he insisted on calling her Miranda. A compromise between Ms Grenville and the 'friendly' diminutive, perhaps. Couldn't he bring himself to be that familiar?

Instead, she said, 'Sure. Consider it a date.'

'It's in my diary,' he assured her, 'but right now we need to move.'

'Yes. Move.'

Having let go once, put on the independent act, Manda found it much harder to prise herself free a second time. That was how it had always been. Pretending once was easy…

He made no attempt to rush her or, impatient, pull away as she slowly prised her fingers free, one at a time. Amazingly, he remained rocklike as she forced herself to peel herself away from the warmth of his body. While she fought the desperate need to throw herself at him as a cold space filled the vacuum where, a moment before, there had been warmth.

Fighting a slide back into the dark sink of desperation, the clinging neediness.

She'd been there and knew how far down it could take her, but it was a tough call. The darkness amplified everything. Not just the tiny sounds, the movements of another person, but the emotion. The fear. And, as she finally let go, mentally casting herself adrift, she sat perfectly still for a moment, taking time to gather herself as Jago moved away from her.

Holding in the scream.

She needed no one. No one…

'Any time in the next ten seconds will do.'

Jago's voice came out of the darkness as astringent as the bitter aloes that one especially hated nanny had painted on her fingernails to stop her biting them. She'd chewed them anyway, refusing to submit, suffering the bitterness to spite the woman. Five years old and even then using her body to take control of her world.

The memory was just the wake-up call she needed and, using the wall as her starting point, she began to edge carefully forward on her hands and knees, casting about in wide sweeps, seeking her bag. Distracting herself from the pain in her knees as she shuffled along the broken floor by thinking about Jago.

So he found her response about trusting a man worthy of derision, did he? It had to mean that some woman had done the dirty on him in the past. The sexy creature selling her dumbed-down book on the ancient Cordilleran civilisation? He'd sounded bitter enough when she'd raised the subject.

She stopped herself from leaping to such obvious conclusions.

To the outside world she had no doubt that her trust problems would have looked that simple, too. Dismissed as the result of a couple of disastrous relationships with men who had commitment problems. She'd seen the grow-up-and-get-over-it looks from people who hadn't a clue.

Nothing was ever that simple.

It wasn't the men. They were no more than a symptom…

She jumped as loose stones fell in a clatter.

'Are you okay?' she asked nervously. What would she do if he wasn't?

'Just peachy,' he replied sarcastically.

Cute. 'You don't actually live down here, do you?' she asked in an effort to keep him talking.

'No. I've got a house down in the village,' he admitted, 'but I keep a camp-bed here. I can get a lot more writing done without the constant interruptions.' His voice seemed to come from miles away. And above her. 'It's about fifteen miles back.'

'Yes, we drove through it.'

She hadn't given a thought to the villagers. She'd seen them working in their tiny fields as they'd driven by. Small children, staring at the bus. Skinny dogs, chickens, goats…

'I hope they're okay down there,' she said.

'Me too, even though they're probably blaming all this on me. Stirring up the old gods. Making them angry.'

'Is that what you've been doing?'

'Not intentionally. They'll have to look further afield for those who've been taking their name in vain.'

Definitely the blonde, then…

'They're not getting excited about the possibility of getting rich off tourism?' she asked.

'The younger ones, maybe. The older people don't want to know.'

'Oh.'

Manda's fingers brushed against something on the floor. A bottle. Glass and, amazingly, intact. She opened it, hoping it was water. She sniffed, blinked. 'I've found your hooch,' she said. 'The bottle wasn't broken.'

'Good. Take care of it.' His voice came from above her. 'We're going to need it.'

She didn't ask why, afraid that she already knew the answer.

CHAPTER SIX

JAGO's foot slipped, dislodging more loose rubble that rattled down to the temple floor, eliciting a small, if quickly contained, cry of alarm from his companion.

'Are you okay?' he asked. The pause was a fraction too long. 'Miranda!'

'Y-yes… Sorry. I thought it was another aftershock.' Then, 'Can you see anything?'

By 'anything' she undoubtedly meant a way out.

'Not a lot,' he replied, relief driving his sarcasm.

He was prodding gently, hoping to find a way through, but having to be careful that he didn't bring the rock ceiling down on top of them. As far as he could tell, however, the far end of the temple where his working supplies were stored was completely blocked off.

Their only escape route appeared to be up through the shaft, always assuming that it hadn't collapsed. He couldn't see the sky. And just for a moment he considered what it would have been like to come round, alone in the darkness, not knowing what had happened.

'I could really do with that light,' he said. Then, 'Any chance in the near future, do you think?' No reply. 'Miranda?'

'I've found my bag.'

She didn't sound happy.

'What's up?'

'Everything is soaking.'

'You can't expect me to get excited about a ruined bag, no matter how expensive.'

'No. It's just… The water bottle split when it fell.'

He just about managed to bite back the expletive that sprang to his lips. It was not good news. 'If there's anything left, drink it now,' he instructed.

'What about you?'

'I'll manage. Just tell me you've found the light.'

In the silence that followed, his mind filled in the blanks; a picture of her tilting her head back as she swallowed, the cool, clean water taking the dust from her mouth.

'What about the damn light, Miranda?' he demanded in an effort to take his mind off it.

In answer, a tiny glow appeared in the darkness.

A really *tiny* glow that did no more than light up the tips of ghostly pink fingers, shimmer off the pale curve of her cheek.

She'd said it was small, but he'd been hoping for one of those small but powerful mini-torches. The kind of sterling silver gizmo that came in expensive Christmas crackers. Women who carried designer bags that had a year-long waiting list didn't buy cheap crackers for their Christmas parties. They bought the kind that contained expensive trinkets for people who had everything. At least they did back in the days when he had been on the guest list.

Maybe she'd gone for some kind of kitsch irony last Christmas because this light must have come out of the budget variety sold in supermarkets, just about powerful enough to illuminate a lock in the dark.

He fought down his disappointment and frustration. This

was not her fault. Miranda Grenville had come out on a sight-seeing trip, not equipped for a survival weekend.

'Well, that's great,' he said, and hoped he sounded as if he meant it. 'I thought it might have been ruined.'

He eased himself back down to the temple floor and carefully made his way across to her with the light as his guide.

'Here,' she said, handing it to him. It went out. 'You have to squeeze the sides to make it work.'

'Very high-tech,' he observed, then wished he'd kept his mouth shut as she found his wrist, slid her fingers down to his hand and guided it to the bottle she was holding.

'Here. I saved you some water. Careful, it's on its side.' Then, before he could take the drink that he was, admittedly, desperate for, she said, 'Wait. I've got some painkillers in here somewhere. For the bump on your head.'

'You don't have faith in the kissing-it-better school of medicine?' he asked, while she fumbled about in the dark for a pack of aspirin, popped a couple of pills from the plastic casing. It was extraordinary how, deprived of sight, the other senses became amplified. How, just by listening, he could tell exactly what she was doing.

'Yes. No…' Then, 'No one ever kissed me better…' she placed the pills into his hand, taking back the light so that he had both hands free to swallow them '…so I couldn't say how effective it is. It's probably wiser to be on the safe side and use the pill popping approach, wouldn't you think?'

He tossed back the pills, swallowed a mouthful of water. 'Never?'

'My family didn't go in for that kind of kissing.'

'No?' His were good at all that stuff. As far as the outside world was concerned, they had been the perfect happy family.

'It's all in the mind,' he said. 'An illusion. If you believe in it, it works.'

'And do you?' she asked. 'Believe?'

'If I say yes, will you kiss me again?'

'I'll take that as a "no".'

Jago wished he'd just said yes, but it was too late for that. 'It got an eight out of ten on the feel-good factor.'

'Only eight?' she demanded.

'You expected a straight ten?' he asked, clearly amused.

In the darkness Manda blushed crimson. Whatever had she been thinking to get into this conversation? Attempting to recover a little self-respect, she said, 'Hardly ten. But taking into account the guesswork involved, the dust, maybe eight point…'

But he didn't wait for her to finish, instead laying his hand against her cheek, brushing his thumb against the edge of her mouth before leaning forward and kissing her back.

Jago's lips were barely more than a breath against her own—a feather-light touch that breathed life, his own warmth into her. Nine point nine recurring…

While she was still trying to gather herself to say something, anything, he saved her from making a total fool of herself and saying that out loud.

'You said you had a phone,' he prompted casually. As if nothing had happened. 'I don't suppose, by any chance, it's the kind that takes photographs?'

Nothing had happened, she reminded herself. He was just trying to keep her from thinking about the situation they were in and she responded with a positively flippant, 'Don't they all?' Then, 'Why? Do you want a souvenir? Pictures to sell to the tabloids.'

'Would the tabloids be that interested?'

Pictures of Miranda Grenville, one-time society hostess,

adviser to the Prime Minister, now businesswomen in her own right, filthy and dishevelled in an underground hell? Oh, yes, they'd love those. But clearly he hadn't a clue who she was and she was happy to leave it that way.

'There's always a market for human interest stories,' she told him as she dug the phone out of her bag, wiped it dry on the sleeve of her shirt and turned it on for the first time since she'd arrived in Cordillera. It lit up, then beeped. 'I've got messages,' she said.

'They'll keep,' Jago replied, taking it from her. 'This is more important. Shut your eyes.'

'Why? What are you—' A bright flash wiped out all the night sight she'd slowly built up. 'Idiot!'

'I told you to shut your eyes,' he said, looking at the image on the screen for a moment before turning slightly. 'And again,' he said.

This time she didn't hesitate as she caught on to what he was doing. With the camera in her cellphone he could take pictures, use them to 'see' exactly what the situation was, maybe find a way out. Or at least locate anything that might be of use to them.

He stared at the third image for so long that she leaned forward to see what held his attention.

'What's that?' she asked, after a moment staring at the picture and trying to make sense of the vast piece of stone that was lying at a broken angle from the floor to the roof.

'The eagle.'

'The one that was part of the ceiling?' she asked, shocked. To see something that huge just tossed aside was chilling.

'I climbed up part of the way just now,' Jago said. The screen lit up the tip of his finger, a short clean nail, as he pointed at the photograph. 'There's a shaft that leads directly out to the forest, but I couldn't find a way through. It may be blocked with debris. Or the eagle might have fallen across it.'

'Oh.'

He took another photograph, and then another. It seemed forever before he grunted with something like satisfaction. 'Keep it pointed that way so that I know how far I've got,' he said, carefully handing her the phone. 'I'll be right back.'

She looked at the photograph, trying to work out what had got him so excited. Had he seen some prospect of escape? No matter how hard she stared, all she could see was a jumble of stone piled almost to the roof.

She heard him pulling at it, the rattle as smaller stones moved. 'Be careful!' Then, letting out a breath of relief as he made his way back to her, 'What was it? What did you see?'

'The handle of a trowel,' he said, passing it to her. It was one of those fine trowels that archaeologists used to scrape away the layers of soil. Pitifully small, but better than nothing. 'Put it in your bag. Did you put the brandy in there?'

'Yes.'

'Good. Put the strap over your head so you don't get parted from it again. There are bound to be more aftershocks.'

He used the same take it or leave it tone with which he'd told her to close her eyes and her first reaction to any kind of order had always been to ignore it. This time, however, she didn't hesitate, putting the trowel in her bag, placing the strap over her head.

And she didn't speak again until he'd painstakingly photographed all three hundred and sixty degrees of what remained of the temple. Kept her bottom lip firmly clamped between her teeth, containing her impatience as he carefully examined each image, instead fixing her gaze on the dark angles and planes of his face in the shadowy light from the small screen. Watching for the slightest sign that he'd found some way out.

Without a word he stopped looking, then turned his attention to the roof and carried on taking photographs.

She did her best to smother a pathetic whimper but he must have heard her because, without pausing in what he was doing, he reached out, found her hand in the faint light from the screen.

He didn't say anything. He didn't have to.

'Well?' she asked, unable to contain herself when, finally, he stopped, looked through all the images and still said nothing.

'Is this you?' he asked.

'What?'

She leaned forward and realised that he'd found the pictures taken at the christening. She'd taken a picture of Belle holding Minette.

'No. That's my sister-in-law. I was godmother to her baby last week.'

'Why do I think I know her?'

'I couldn't say,' she replied, unwilling to add glamour to her sister-in-law by telling him that, until recently, she had been the nation's breakfast television sweetheart. 'Maybe you've a thing for voluptuous women?'

'If I have, believe me I'm over it. What about this?' he asked, flipping on to the next picture.

'That's Daisy. She's my assistant. My sister-in-law's sister. It was a joint christening and I was godmother to her little boy too.'

'So where's number three?'

'Three?'

'Doesn't everything come in threes? Wishes? Disasters? Babies…'

'Not in this family,' she said sharply.

'That would be the family you're taking a break from?'

Had she really said that? To this total stranger. Except that when a man had kissed you—twice—he could hardly be described as a stranger. Even when you didn't know what he looked like. Anything about him. Except that he knew when to be tough and when to be gentle. And when a girl needed a hand to hold in the dark.

Maybe that was enough.

'The same family whose photographs you carry about with you?'

'It's…complicated.'

'Families usually are,' he said with feeling.

'What about you? Will your family be glued to the twenty-four hour news channels? Or flying out to help in the search?'

'It's unlikely. They have no idea I'm in Cordillera.'

'Really? I assumed you'd been here for quite a while.'

'Nearly five years.'

'Oh.'

'We're not what you could call close.'

'I'm sorry.'

'It's my choice.'

'Right.' Then, 'Mine don't know, either. Where I am.'

'You said.'

She had said rather a lot for such a short acquaintance, but then the circumstances had an intensity that speeded up the normal course of social intercourse.

'Of course I've only been gone a few days,' she added, feeling guilty.

'I'm sure you'd have got around to sending a postcard eventually.'

'I don't send postcards.'

'Or call? They seem to have been calling you.'

'Those messages? Probably business,' she said dismissively. 'Belle and Daisy and I have a television production company. We're due to start work on a new documentary soon.'

'Oh, well, the good news is that we needn't worry about them worrying about us.'

That was the *good* news?

'Okay, Miranda Grenville. We seem to have just two options. I may have found a way through the roof. The first part of the climb would be fairly easy. Up the back of the eagle where it's sloping to the ground. But after that it's going to be a tough climb, finding footholds in the dark. See?'

He showed her the picture of a dark gash in the roof where the light hadn't reflected back, suggesting space.

'Unfortunately I can't say what we'll find when we get there. We might still be—'

'What's the alternative?' she asked.

'We could try and clear this corner.' He flipped forward to a photograph that showed a corner where the wall had subsided. 'The ground falls away there, so it's unlikely to be blocked with debris once we're through.'

'If we can get through,' she said.

'If we can get through,' he confirmed. 'The third option is to stay put and hope that the sniffer dogs are on their way.'

'I don't think I'll hold my breath on that one.' Manda did her best to swallow down the fear. 'I imagine they already have their paws full.' She tried not to think about what was going on outside. The suffering… 'Which would you choose? If you didn't have to think about me?'

There was a telling pause before he said, 'I think clearing the corner might be the most sensible option.'

He was lying.

'If you were on your own you'd go for the climb. Admit it.'

He hesitated a fraction too long before saying, 'In the dark it could be suicide.'

'You think I'm not up to it, is that it?'

'I've no idea what you're up to, but it's not that. If there's a shock while we're up there—'

'Shut up, Jago.'

'Miranda…'

'If there's a shock it could all come down on top of us.' He didn't say anything. 'And climbing would be quicker.'

'True,' he admitted. 'Did you say something about a packet of mints? Or did they dissolve when the water leaked?'

'You're in luck, they're the chewy kind.' She felt around in her bag until she found them, unwrapped two mints and handed him one. Then she snapped the rest of the pack in two and gave half to him. 'Here. Don't eat them all at once.'

'No, ma'am,' he replied and her eyes were now so accustomed to the low light levels emitting from the phone that she clearly saw him tuck the sweets into his shirt pocket. 'Okay, here's the plan. I'll go up and take a look to see if it's possible, then I'll come back for you.'

'Leaving me down here? No way!'

'You want your mints back?' he asked.

'Stuff the mints…' She didn't care a fig about them. 'Stuff you.' He wasn't going to abandon her. 'Give me my phone back and I'll find my own way.'

As she made a grab for it, he moved it out of reach. 'You think I'd abandon you?'

'Not intentionally. But once you're up there…' He'd be exhausted. It would take a superhero to climb back down into the dark. Not that it mattered. It wasn't going to happen.

'Let's just say that experience has led me to have very low expectations of the average male.'

'Then it's your lucky day. The one thing I'm not is average.'

'No?' Actually, she probably thought he was right, but she wasn't about to pander to his ego. 'So where do you fit? Above or below the median?'

'You'd better hope that it's above.'

'I'll let you know.'

'Cat,' he replied, but softly so that she was sure he was smiling. Then, leaning into her so that she could see the screen, 'Okay. This is the way we go,' he said, pointing out the route he'd chosen.

'What about this way?' she suggested, pointing to what looked like a fissure. 'It looks easier.'

'Did I ask your opinion?'

'But—'

'This isn't a committee, lady.' She hadn't realised the voice could reflect the expression so clearly, but it was obvious that he wasn't smiling now. 'Pay close attention because I'm going to say this just once, then I'm going, with you or without you.'

Damn...

She hadn't meant to do that. It wasn't that she doubted him or his good intentions but she was so used to people listening to her opinions. Being in control...

Whatever he thought, he didn't wait for her to answer one way or the other but, having made his point, he looped his arm over her and pulled her closer. Then, with her chin pressed against his shoulder—she hadn't imagined the strength—he laid out the route they'd take, pointing out crevices for hands and feet that she'd never have seen. Finally, when he was done, he took her hand and placed the phone into her palm, pressing her fingers around it.

'You should keep it,' she said. Doing her best to make up for… Well, just about everything.

'Probably,' he admitted, wrapping her fingers around it. 'Keep it safe.'

His way of proving that she could trust him not to abandon her? Or, having picked out his escape route was he simply freeing up his hands for the climb?

It didn't matter, she decided, as she slipped it into the large breast pocket of her shirt where it would be easily accessible. Then she looked up into the dark void and knew exactly what he'd done.

He'd given her the best light source in case she needed it to find her way and, feeling really bad for doubting him, she said, 'Here, take the mini-light.'

'Sure?'

She didn't answer, but pressed it into his palm. Then, as he turned it on to light his way, she looked up. 'How high is it?'

'Just be grateful these people didn't build on the scale of the Egyptians,' he replied, evading the question.

'How high?' she insisted.

'About ten metres,' he replied, far too glibly, not looking back.

'Don't patronise me, Jago.'

He was close enough for her to feel him shrug, then he turned slightly so that she could see his spare, finely chiselled profile. 'Does it matter?' he asked.

'I like to be in possession of all the facts.'

'A bit of a control freak, are you?'

'Not at all. You can ask anyone. I'm a *total* control freak.'

'Then here are the facts for you. We start at the bottom and we keep going until we reach the top. Simple.' Then, 'What did you do with that bottle of brandy?'

'Need a stiffener before you face it?' she asked, passing it to him.

The light went out and she heard him unscrew the cap. 'Give me your hands.'

About to ask why, she thought better of it and held them out without a word as he placed one of his own beneath them. Then he poured the spirit over both of their hands and she let slip something brief and scatological as the spirit found its way into the scrapes and grazes, bringing tears to her eyes.

'Antiseptic,' he said. 'And it'll dry out your skin. Help with grip.'

'Thanks,' she said cryptically.

'Don't mention it.' He tucked the bottle back into the bag hanging from her back, then said, 'You'd better give me that.'

'Are you sure about that? It'll be a bad look,' she warned as she lifted the strap over her head and surrendered it to him. 'It definitely won't match your shoes.'

'You know that for a fact, do you?'

'I can't believe you're wearing silver sandals.'

'Please tell me you're kidding.' Then, 'No. Don't say another word. I'd rather not know.'

He didn't wait but, using the small light, he began to move away from her. Having mentally slapped herself on the wrist for being a bad girl—but honestly, any man who seriously believed any girl with a grain of sense would wear silver sandals in the rainforest deserved to be teased—she began to follow him, further scuffing the toes of her expensive loafers as she crawled after him on her hands and knees.

Sensible, after all, did not have to be cheap. Or lack style.

Ahead of her, Jago stood up, turning back to take her arm and help her to her feet. About to remind him that she could manage, she felt her knee buckle slightly. Muffled by all the other aches and pains she was suffering, she'd forgotten about her knee.

'Okay?'

'Fine.' There was a long moment of silence and she knew he was looking at her, trying to gauge just how fine she really was. 'Absolutely dandy,' she assured him. 'No problem. How's your head?'

'I'll live.' Then, 'Let's get on with it.'

In the darkness she found her ears filling in the pictures; the sound of cloth brushing against skin as he moved, of muscles stretching as he reached up, using the tiny light to illuminate the first of the hand-holds that he'd pinpointed on the photograph. Then everything went dark again.

He didn't begin to climb away from her, however, but reached back and found her hand, lifting it to a narrow crack so that she could feel it for herself, would know how far to stretch, what she was looking for. Have a starting point.

'Got that?' he asked.

'Got it,' she assured him.

'Okay. We'll take it one move at a time. I'll give you a running commentary of my moves so that you can follow them.' Then, 'We're climbing blind and it's not going to be easy and it's not going to be quick. Stop for rests whenever you need to. Don't try to rush it.'

'Yes, sir.'

She didn't actually leap to attention and salute, but the voice implied it and he didn't actually sigh. His momentary pause was enough.

'I hear you, Jago,' she added quickly, wanting him to know that she was with him every step of the way.

'Right.' Then, 'Whatever you do, don't panic. If you're in trouble, tell me. I'd rather come back a few feet to give you a hand than climb back down to the bottom after listening to you scream all the way down.'

She swallowed, lifted her chin.

'If it helps,' she replied, 'you have my promise that I'll do my best not to scream.'

CHAPTER SEVEN

MANDA bit back a yelp as her hand slipped, scraping her knuckles against sharp stone.

It had seemed easy enough at first. The back of the eagle had formed a slope, a fairly steep one, and there were plenty of hand-holds—fissures, small ledges just big enough for her feet, where it had cracked as it had fallen.

But then they reached the wall itself and the climb became harder. Her muscles began to burn with the effort of pulling herself up, her arms to shake and it soon became obvious that all the hand-holds in the world wouldn't get her to the top if she didn't have the strength to hold on.

Breathing was becoming a problem too, her chest aching with the strain. Only by concentrating on the calm, steady voice of Jago, guiding her onwards and upwards, was she able to block out the worst of it. Keep moving.

She didn't manage to completely stifle her difficulty in breathing, however, and finally he paused above her and said, 'Are you okay?'

'Peachy,' she managed, going for sarcasm in an attempt to disguise her pain.

'There's a good ledge here. We'll take a rest…'

'Right.' Excellent. Except that her fingers were numb and

she didn't have the strength to move. Instead, she leaned her face against the cold, damp rock wall.

'A couple of feet,' he prompted.

Forget the comfort of the ancient leather sofa in the Belgravia mansion that she had, until recently, called home, his rock ledge sounded like heaven right now.

And about as close…

Above her, small stones were dislodged from the wall and for a moment she thought that he was moving on without her.

'Jago…'

Even as the word was involuntarily torn from her he was at her side, his arm, then his body at her back, holding her tight against the wall. Taking the strain.

'Let go,' he said, his mouth so close to her ear that his neck was tight against her head, his breath, no more than a gasp, warm against her cheek. 'I've got you.'

'I can't…'

'Trust me.'

How many times had she heard those words? How many times had they been hollow lies?

'I'm okay,' she told him, hating this. 'Just catching my breath.' She hated being weak, hated needing a prop. Just once she yearned to be the strong one, but she did as she was told, flexing her fingers, so that the blood flowed, painfully, back into them.

'Where did you put your mints?'

'What's the matter? Have you eaten all yours?'

Jago shifted, crushing her against the temple wall as he struggled to reach his own, slipping the wrapper with his thumb, praying that they weren't sugar free—how likely was that?—as he found her lips.

'Take it!' he said, but instead of just doing as she was told, she bit it in two, leaving half behind for him. Always having to have the last word… 'Miranda!'

'Shares…' she gasped, and Jago didn't have the breath to argue, but palmed it into his mouth before grabbing for a small crevice in the wall, his muscles screaming as he bore her weight as well as his own for what seemed like hours.

In reality it was only seconds before she said, 'Okay. I've got it now.'

'Sure? If you can just make the next move…'

'Go!'

Tough. Foolhardy. Determined not to slow him down. Miranda Grenville might be the most irritating woman he'd ever met, but she still earned his grudging respect as he edged carefully back to his original position on the ledge.

He reached out instinctively to grab her as he heard her foot slip, her grunt as some part of her anatomy collided painfully with stone, afraid that her mouth had finally outreached her strength.

All he got was a handful of air and then, somehow, she was there, alongside him.

'Shall we go mad and have another mint?' he asked.

'My treat,' she managed, biting one of her own in half and sharing it with him.

They both sat there for a while, side by side, their backs against the temple wall, chewing slowly while their breathing recovered and the feeling began to flow back into tortured limbs.

From above them a few small stones rattled down the face and Manda stopped breathing as Jago threw his arm across her, pinning her back against the wall, waiting for another aftershock.

Waited. And waited.

Finally she shuddered as she let out the breath she was

holding and Jago slumped against her. 'A bird,' he said. 'It must have been a bird. Good news. If a bird can get in, we can get out.'

'Sure,' Manda agreed.

She wasn't entirely convinced. The bird could have been trapped like them. Or it could be a bat. One of those big, hairy, fruit-eating bats...

'Why don't you talk to your family?' she asked, into his neck, not wanting to think about bats, or what else might be tucked up with them. Lurking in the crevices into which she was blindly poking her fingers. Not wanting him to move. Wanting to stay exactly where they were.

His only response was to remove the arm he'd thrown protectively across her and say, 'We'd better get on.' But even as he made a move she caught at his sleeve.

'Tell me!' Then, shocked at herself, knowing that she could never talk about her own miserable childhood, she apologised. 'I'm sorry.'

'It's okay. I'll tell you when we get out of here. Over a cold beer.'

'Another date?'

'It sounds like it.'

The climb was both mentally and physically exhausting. Feeling in the dark for each hold, convinced that every dislodged stone was a new tremor, Jago's worst fear was that he'd reach up in the darkness and find only chiselled-smooth rock.

He'd done some rock climbing as a young man and field archaeology was for the fit, but he understood why Miranda wouldn't wait for him to make the climb, find help and come back for her.

He didn't think he could have remained at the bottom in the darkness either, but with every move he was waiting for the slip behind him, tensed for her cry. He was unable to do anything but keep going and guide her to his own footholds. Praying that he wasn't just leading her into a dead end.

At least she was listening, didn't panic when she couldn't immediately locate the next hand- or foot-hold.

'How're you doing?' he asked.

If it had been physically possible, Manda would have laughed.

Doing? *Doing?* Was he kidding?

A muttered, 'Fine…' stretched her ability to speak to the limit.

It was a lie. She wasn't 'fine'. Not by any definition of the word.

The muscles in her shoulders, arms, back were quivering with exhaustion. Forget the 'burn'. Her calves and thighs were on fire and she couldn't feel her feet. She was just moving on automatic.

Then, as her fingers, wet with sweat—or blood—slipped, her forehead came into sharp contact with smooth stone and for a moment everything spun in the dark. As she sucked air into her lungs, hanging on with what felt like the ends of her fingernails, she managed to gasp, 'If I fall you're not to climb down.'

He'd stopped moving. 'You're not going to fall.'

'Promise me,' she demanded. 'You have to get out. I want my family to know what happened to me.'

'Like I could look them in the eye and tell them I'd left you lying on the floor of the temple, not knowing if you were dead or alive.' His breath was coming hard too. 'Stop gassing and move. You're nearly there.'

'Of course I am,' she muttered. Did he think she was totally stupid?

'Reach out with your left foot and you'll find a good

ledge. Carefully!' he warned, as she felt for the ledge, thought she had it, only for it to crumble away, leaving her scrabbling for purchase. What was left of her nails scraped across chiselled-smooth stone as she fought to hang on, suspended by one toe and raw fingertips over a blackness that seemed to be sucking her down.

She'd been there so many times in her head but this was real. This time she really was going down and never coming up again. All she had to do was let go…

'Stop pussy-footing about and move, woman!' Jago's harsh voice echoed around the ruined temple, jerking her back. How dared he?

Ivo had never shouted at her. He'd been gentle. Coaxing her back from the brink…

'Any time in the next ten seconds will do!'

But anger was good, too…

'You pig!' she cried, as her toe finally connected with something solid, but her leg was trembling so much that she couldn't make the move.

'Come up here and tell me that!'

'What's the matter, Jago? Are you in a hurry for another kick?'

'Looking forward to it, sweetheart!'

'I'm on my way!'

'Promises, promises. Are you ready for another kiss?'

The adrenalin rush got her across and she didn't wait for him to guide her, but reached up, seeking the next move without waiting for guidance. She'd survived her moment of panic. The black moment when falling would have been a relief.

She'd come through…

He'd brought her through.

Jago.

'The next bit is a bit of a stretch,' he said as she groped in the darkness for a hold in the darkness. 'Reach up and I'll pull you over the edge.'

Edge? She'd been that close?

And now she was out here alone?

Without warning, the blackness sucked at her and she made a desperate lunge upwards, seeking his hand. For a moment his fingers brushed tantalisingly against hers.

She was alone. Out of reach…

'It's too far…'

'Hold on.' She was showered with a fine film of dust as he moved closer to the edge above her. 'Okay. Try again.'

His palm touched hers. Slipped.

He grunted as he grabbed for her wrist, his fingers biting hard as he held her.

'Give me your other hand,' he gasped.

Let go?

Put her life entirely in his hands?

In the millisecond she hesitated, another aftershock ripped through the wall and the ledge on which she was standing gave way beneath her, tearing her hand away from the wall so that she was left hanging over the empty temple.

Somehow, Jago managed to hang on, his arm practically torn from its socket as he stretched out over the chasm, taking her full weight with one hand as Miranda struggled to find some kind of footing. Slipping closer and closer towards the tipping point when they'd both fall.

Stone was crashing around them, filling the air with dust. Something—someone—was screaming. Then, mercifully, the shaking stopped, Miranda's feet connected with something solid and, bracing her feet against the wall, between them they managed to get her over the edge.

He caught her, rolling away with her from the precipice, holding her, even as the pain exploded in his shoulder, his head. As her voice exploded in his ear.

'Idiot!'

'Without a doubt,' he managed as she sucked in a breath, presumably to continue berating him. The dust caught in her throat and she began to cough. Not that she let a little thing like that stop her.

'Don't you ever do that again!'

'I promise.' He might have laughed if it didn't hurt so much. Maybe it was hurting so much because he was laughing, he couldn't tell.

'I mean it! I'm not worth dying for, do you hear me?'

He heard her, heard a raw pain as the words were wrenched from her. It wasn't just reaction, he realised. Or shock.

She truly meant what she'd said and, despite his own physical pain, he wrapped his arms around her and held her close even though she fought him like a tiger. Held her safe until she stopped telling him over and over, 'I'm not worth it…'

Until she let go, subsided against his chest and only the slightest movement of her shoulders betrayed that she was weeping.

It was her struggle to conceal the hot tears soaking into his shirt as they lay huddled together on the earth that finally got to him.

She had every right to howl, stamp, scream her head off after what she'd been through. She certainly hadn't shown any reticence when it came to expressing her feelings until now. In truth, he would have welcomed the promised kick, or at least a mouthful of abuse. Anything that would stop him from asking her why she wasn't worth dying for.

He didn't want to know. Didn't want to get that involved.

But, even as he fought it, he recognised, somewhere, deep

down, that it was a forlorn hope. Her life belonged to him, as his belonged to her.

From the moment he'd reached out in the dark and his hand had connected with this woman, their survival had been inextricably linked. Whatever happened in the future, this day, these few hours would, forever, bind them together.

And they were not home free yet. Not by a long way.

'Hey, come on. No need for that,' he said, tugging out the tail of his shirt and using it to wipe her face, as she'd used hers to wipe the dust from his in what now seemed like a lifetime ago.

Kissing her cheek. Kissing her better.

'Don't!'

His kiss was almost more than she could bear. The gentle innocence of it. Almost as if she were a child. It nearly undid all his good work in putting her back together. It took what little remained of Manda's self-control to stop herself from grasping handfuls of Jago's shirt, holding on to the solid human warmth of his body. Clinging to the safety net that he seemed to offer.

'Enough,' she said, scrubbing at her face with her sleeve to eradicate the softness of his shirt against her skin. The softness of his lips.

Wiping out all evidence of her own pitiful weakness.

She hadn't cried in years. She'd been so sure there were no more tears left in her. But this stranger had risked his own life to save her...

'You should have let me fall,' she said. 'I told you to let—'

'Next time,' he cut in, stopping the words.

Damn him, she meant it!

She closed her eyes in an attempt to stop more tears from spilling down her cheeks, took a breath, then, when she could trust herself to speak, said, 'Is that a promise?'

'It's a promise.'

'Right. Well, okay… Good.'

'You have my word that the very next time you're climbing the wall of the inner sanctum of the Temple of Fire you're on your own.'

'What? No!'

'Isn't that what you meant?'

'You know it isn't. We're not out of here yet and what's the point of us both dying?'

'No one is going to die,' he replied with a sudden fierceness. 'Not today. Not here. Not in my temple.'

'I wish I had your confidence.'

'You've got something better, much better than that, Miranda Grenville. You've got me.'

It was a totally outrageous thing to say, Jago knew. His shoulder was practically useless and the headache that had never entirely eased was now back with a vengeance. But a spluttering laugh that she couldn't quite hold in reassured him.

'So I have. While you, poor sap, are stuck with me. Useless at taking orders and with a trust threshold hovering on zero.' With that she stilled. 'I could have got us both killed back there.'

'Don't beat yourself up about it. We react in the way we're programmed to.'

'And you're programmed to be the hero.' She laid her hand against his chest. 'Thank you for holding on.' Then, as if embarrassed by her own gratitude, she said, 'So? What next, fearless leader? We're not out of the woods yet.'

He caught her hand before she could move and lay back, taking her with him. Closing his eyes. 'We rest. Try and get some sleep.'

'Sleep?'

'What's up, princess? Missing your silk sheets and goose down pillows?'

'Silk sheets? Please…' But she shivered.

'You're cold?'

'Not cold, although it is colder up here. There's more air, too. Do you think there's a way out?'

'Part of the roof has gone. Look, you can see a few stars.'

'Oh…' Then, eagerly, 'Can't we press on?'

'We need to recover a little before we attempt another climb,' he said. He needed to recover. 'And when the eagle collapsed it took part of the floor at this level with it. It seems solid enough here, but…'

'We could take more pictures.'

'If we wait, we'll have daylight,' he said. 'There's no point in taking any risks.'

'I'm not sure about that. It's easier to be brave when you can't see the danger.'

'Trust me.'

'You keep saying that.' She shrugged. 'I guess it makes sense,' she said, but not with any real enthusiasm and who could blame her? 'It's just this place. It gives me the creeps.'

'Afraid of the dark?' He released her hand. 'Come on, cooch up,' he said, holding out his arm so that she could curl up against him, 'and I'll tell you a bedtime story.' She ignored the offered comfort, keeping her distance. He went ahead with the story, anyway. Telling her about the people who'd built the temple. The way they'd lived. What they had worshipped.

He thought she'd be happier if she knew that they didn't go into for bloody sacrifice. That their 'fire' was not a thing to fear. How, when the moon was full, they'd built a fire on the altar at the heart of their temple, then heaped the huge night-scented lilies that bloomed in the forest on to the embers so that the eagle could catch the sweet smoke that was carried up the shaft and fly with it in his wings as a gift to the moon.

'How can you know all that?' she asked in wonder.

'They carved pictures into the walls, drew their ceremonies in pictograms. And laboratories have analysed the ashes we found under centuries of compacted leaf litter.'

'But that's really beautiful, Jago. Why didn't the guide tell us all this?'

'Because the guide doesn't know. I haven't published any of my findings.'

'But what about—'

'Enough.' He didn't want to think about Fliss. He was angry with her, angry with Felipe, but most of all he was angry with himself. This was his fault. If he hadn't been so stubborn, so intent to keeping the world he'd uncovered for himself… 'It's your turn,' he said. 'Tell me what you're running away from.'

CHAPTER EIGHT

'Who said I was running away?' she demanded.

'"Time out"?' Jago offered, quoting her own words back at her. 'That's a euphemism if ever I heard one. Not checking your messages? Not sending postcards home?'

She drew in a long slow breath and for a moment he thought she was going to tell him to get lost. That it was none of his business. But she didn't. She didn't say anything at all for a long time and when, finally, she did break the silence, it was with just one word.

'Myself.'

'What?'

He'd been imagining a job fiasco, a family row, a messy love affair. Maybe all three.

'All my life I've been running away from this horrible creature that no one could love.'

It was, Jago thought, one of those 'sod it' moments.

Like that time when he was a kid and had poked a stick into a hollow tree and disturbed a wasps' nest. It was something you really, really wished you hadn't done, but there was no escaping the consequences.

'No one?' he asked.

Her shoulders shifted imperceptibly. Except that everything was magnified by the darkness.

'Ivo, my brother, did his best to take care of me. In return I came close to dragging him to the brink with me. Something I seem to be making a habit of.' There was a pause, this time no more than a heartbeat. 'Although on that occasion I was in mental, rather than physical, freefall.'

'You had a breakdown?'

'That's what they called it. The doctors persuaded him to section me. Confine me under the Mental Health Act for my own safety.'

And suddenly he wasn't thinking *sod it*. He was only thinking how hard it must be for her to say that to a stranger. Actually, how hard it would be to say that to someone she knew well.

Mental illness was the last taboo.

'You both survived,' he said, mentally freewheeling while he tried to come up with something appropriate. 'At least I assume your brother did, since you've just been godmother to his sprog. And, for that matter, so did you.'

'Yes, he survived—he's incredibly strong—but it hurt him, having to do that.'

And then, as if suddenly aware of what she was doing, how she was exposing herself, she tried to break free, stand up, distance herself from him.

'Don't!' he warned, sitting up too quickly in his attempt to stop her. His head swam. His shoulder protested. 'Don't move! The last thing I need is for you to fall back down into that damn hole.' Then, because he knew it would get her when kindness wouldn't, 'I'd only have to climb all the way back down and pick up the pieces.'

'I told you—'

'I know. You fall, I'm to leave you to rot. Sorry, I couldn't do that any more than your brother could.'

For a moment she remained where she was, halfway between sitting and standing, but they both knew it was just pride keeping her on her feet and, after a moment, she sank back down beside him.

'You remembered,' she said.

'You make one hell of an impression.'

'Do I?' She managed a single snort of amusement. 'Well, I've had years of practice. I started young, honing my skills on nannies. I caused riots at kindergarten—'

'Riots? Dare I ask?'

'I don't know. How do you feel about toads? Spiders? Ants?'

'I can take them or leave them,' he said. 'Ants?'

'Those great big wood ants.'

'What a monster you were.'

'I did my best,' she assured him. 'I actually managed to get expelled from three prep schools before I discovered that was a waste of time since, if your family has enough money, the right contacts, there is always another school. That there's always some secretary to lumber with the task…'

'You didn't like school?'

'I loved it,' she said. 'Getting thrown out is what's known as cutting off your nose to spite your face.'

In other words, he thought, crying out for attention from the people who should have been there for her. And, making the point that whatever happened he would be there for her, he put his arm around her, wincing under cover of darkness as he eased himself back against the wall, pulling her up against his shoulder.

'Are you okay, Jago?'

She might not be able to see him wince, but she must have heard the catch in his breath.

'Fine,' he lied. Then, because he needed a distraction, 'Ivo?' It wasn't exactly a common name. 'Your brother's name is Ivo Grenville?'

'Ivan George Grenville, to be precise.' She sighed. 'Financial genius. Philanthropist. Adviser to world statesmen. No doubt you've heard of him. Most people have.'

'Actually I was thinking about a boy with the same name who was a year below me at school. Could he be your brother? His parents never came to take him out. Not even to prize-giving the year he won—'

'Not even the year he won the Headmaster's Prize,' she said. 'Yes. That would be Ivo.'

'Clever bugger. My parents were taking me out somewhere for a decent feed and I felt so sorry for him I was going to ask him if he wanted to come along.'

'But you didn't.'

'How do you know that?'

'I wasn't criticising you, Jago. It's just that I know my brother. He never let anyone get that close. Not even me. Not until he met Belle. He's different now.'

'Well, good. I'm sorry I let him put me off.'

He'd meant to keep an eye out for him, but there had been so many other things to fill the days and even a single year's age gap seemed like a lifetime at that age.

'Don't blame yourself. Ivo's way of dealing with our parents' rejection was to put up a wall of glass. No inter-action, no risk of getting hurt. Mine, on the other hand, was to create havoc in an attempt to force them to notice me.'

'That I can believe. What did you do once you'd run out of the livestock option? Kick the headmistress?'

'Are you ever going to let me forget that?'

'Never,' he said, and the idea of teasing her about that for the next fifty years gave him an oddly warm feeling. Stupid. In fifty hours from now they would have gone on their separate ways, never to see one another again. Instead, he concentrated on what really mattered. 'Tell me about your parents. Why did they reject you both?'

'Oh, that's much too strong a word for it. Rejection would have involved serious effort and they saved all their energy for amusing themselves.'

'So why bother—to have children?'

'Producing offspring, an heir and a spare, even if the spare turned out to be annoyingly female, was expected of them. The Grenville name, the future of the estate had to be taken care of.'

'Of course. Stupid of me,' he said sarcastically.

'It's what they had been brought up to, Jago. Generations of them. On one side you have Russian royalty who never accepted that the world had changed. On the other, the kind of people who paid other people to run their houses, take care of their money and, duty done, rear their children. They had more interesting, more important things to do.'

What could ever be more important than kissing your kid better when she grazed a knee? Jago wondered. The memory of his own mother kissing his four-year-old elbow after he'd fallen from his bike sprang, unbidden, to his mind. How she'd smiled as she'd said, 'All better.' Told him how brave he was...

He shut it out.

'Chillingly selfish,' he said, 'but at least it was an honest response. At least they didn't pretend.'

'Pretence would have required an effort.' She lifted her head to look up at him. 'Is that what your parents did, Jago? Pretend?'

Her question caught him on the raw. He didn't talk about his family. He'd walled up that part of his life. Shut it away.

Until the scent of rosemary had stirred a memory of a boy and his bicycle…

Lies, lies, lies…

'Jago?'

She said his name so softly, but even that was a lie. Not his real name. They were alone together, locked in a dark and broken world, reliant upon one another for their very survival and she had a right to his name.

'Nick,' he said.

'Nick…'

It was so long since anyone had called him that. The soft sound of her voice saying his name ripped at something inside him and he heard himself say, 'I was in my final year at uni when I was door-stepped by a journalist.'

She took the hand that he'd hooked around her waist to keep her close and the words, coiled up inside him, began to unravel…

He could see the man now. The first to reach his door. He hadn't introduced himself, not wanting to put him on his guard. He'd just said his name. 'Nick?' And when he'd said, 'Yes…' he'd just pitched in with, 'What's your reaction to the rumour…'

'My father was a politician,' he said. 'A member of the Government. A journalist knocked on my door one day and asked me if I knew my father had been having a long-term affair with a woman in his London office. One of his researchers. That I had a fourteen-year-old half-sister…'

He caught himself. He didn't talk about them, ever.

'Oh, Nick…' She said his name again, softly, echoing his pain. He shouldn't have told her. No one else had used it in fifteen years and to hear it spoken that way caught at feelings he'd buried so deep that he'd forgotten how much they hurt. How betrayed he'd felt. How lost.

'That was when I discovered that all that "happy families" stuff was no more than window-dressing.'

She didn't say she was sorry, just moved a little closer in the dark. It was enough.

'It must have been a big story at the time,' she said after a while, 'but I don't recall the name.'

'It was fifteen years ago. No doubt you were still at school.'

'I suppose, even so—'

'A juicy political scandal is hard to miss.'

It hadn't just been the papers. His father had been the poster boy for the perfect marriage, a solid family life. It had brought out the whole media wolf pack and the television satirists had had a field day.

'You're right, of course. The fact is that I don't use his name any more. Neither of us do. My father was dignified, my mother stood by him and, in the fullness of time, he was rewarded for a lifetime of commitment to his country, his party, with a life peerage. Or maybe the title was my mother's reward for all those years of keeping up appearances, playing the perfect constituency wife. Not making a fuss. But then why would she?'

It was obvious that she'd always known about the affair, the child, but she had enjoyed her life too much to give it up. Had chosen to look the other way and live with it.

'She was the one who spent weekends at the Prime Minister's home in the country,' he said. 'Went on the foreign tours. Enjoyed all the perks of his position. Got the title.'

'What did they say to you?'

He shook his head. 'I went home, expecting to find my mother in bits, my father ashamed, packing.' It had taken the police presence to get him through the television crews and the press pack blocking the lane, but inside the house it was as if nothing had changed. 'It was just another day in politics and they assumed I'd come down to put on a united family front. Go out with them for the photo call. My mother was furious with me for refusing to play the game. She said I owed my father total loyalty. That the country needed him.'

He could still see the two of them going out to face the cameras together, the smiling arm-in-arm pose by the garden gate with the dogs that had made the front page of all the newspapers the next day. Could still smell the rosemary as the photographers had jostled for close-ups, hoping to catch the pain and embarrassment behind the composed smiles. As if…

'What I hated most, couldn't forgive,' he said, 'was the way the other woman was treated like a pariah. Frozen out. She had to give up her job, go into hiding, take out an injunction against the press to protect her daughter. Start over somewhere new.'

'You don't blame her at all? She wasn't exactly innocent, Nick, and someone must have leaked the information to the press. Maybe she hoped to force your father's hand.'

'If she did she was a fool,' he said dismissively.

'She didn't go for the kiss-and-tell? Even then?'

'No. Everyone behaved impeccably. Kept their mouths shut and my father was back in government before the year was over.'

'She loved him, then.'

'I imagine so. She was a fool twice over.'

'I suppose.' Miranda's shivering little sigh betrayed her. Was that how she saw herself? A fool?

'If it wasn't for herself, maybe it was for her daughter.'

She swallowed nervously, as if aware of treading on dangerous ground.

'Perhaps she wanted some of what you had,' she said when he didn't respond. 'To be publicly acknowledged by her father. In her place…'

'In her place, what?' he demanded when she faltered.

'It's what I would have done,' she admitted.

'Poking a stick into a wasps' nest,' he said, realising that she was probably right. 'Poor kid.'

'She's a woman, Jago. About my age. Your sister. And you're wrong about your parents losing nothing,' she said before he could tell her that he didn't have a sister. That she was nothing to him. 'They lost you.'

'The people I thought were my parents didn't exist. Their entire life was a charade.'

'Truly? All of it? Even when they came to your school open day?'

'They did what was expected of them, Miranda,' he said, refusing to give them credit for anything. 'It was just another photo op. Like going to church when they were in the constituency. Pure hypocrisy. It didn't mean anything.'

She sucked in her breath as if about to say something, then thought better of it. 'You changed your name? Afterwards?'

'I use my grandfather's name. Part of it, anyway. He emigrated from eastern Europe. Nothing as grand as Russian royalty, you understand, just a young man trying to escape poverty. They put him off the boat at the first port they came to and told him he was in America. We have a lot in common.'

'Don't you think—'

'No,' he said abruptly. 'I don't.' It was the last thing he wanted to think about. 'What about you? Do you see your parents these days? Did they manage to find time for their granddaughter's christening?'

She shook her head, then, realising that he couldn't see, said, 'They died in an accident years ago. When Ivo was just out of university and I was in sixth form taking my A levels.'

Jago found himself in the unusual situation of not having a clue what to say.

To offer sympathy for the loss of parents who had never been there for her would have been as hypocritical as anything his parents had ever done. Saying what was expected. Hollow words. Yet he knew there would still be an emptiness. A space that nothing could ever fill…

'How did you cope?' he asked finally.

Manda caught a yawn. She ached everywhere, her hands were sore, her mouth gluey. The only comfort was the heat of Jago's shoulder beneath her head. His arm keeping her close. His low husky voice drowning out the small noises, the scuffling, that she didn't want to think about.

'Everything suddenly landed on Ivo's shoulders. He'd been about to take a year off to travel. Instead, he found himself having to deal with all the consequences of unexpected death. Step up and take over. He was incredible.'

'I don't doubt it, but I was asking about you. Singular.'

'Oh.' How rare was that…? 'I suppose the hardest thing was having to accept that, no matter what I did, how good I was, or how bad, my mother and father were never going to turn up, hold me, tell me that it was going to be all right because they loved me.'

It was all she'd ever wanted.

'And?' he said, dragging her back from the moment she'd stood at their graveside, loving them and hating them in the same breath.

She wished she could see him. See his eyes, read him… Cut off from all those visual signals that she could read like a book, she was lost. And in the dark she couldn't use that cool, dismissive smile she'd perfected for when people got too close. The one that Ivo said was like running into a brick wall.

She had no mask to hide behind.

'There must have been an "and",' he persisted. 'You're not the kind of woman who just sits back and takes it.'

'Not only a hero but smart with it,' she said, letting her head fall back against this unexpected warmth that had nothing to do with temperature.

No visual clues, but his voice was as rich and comforting as a mouthful of her sister-in-law's chocolate cake. And, like that sinful confection, to be taken only in very small quantities because the comfort glow was an illusion.

She wasn't fooling herself. The magic would fade with the dawn as such things always did in fairy stories, but for now, in the dark, with his shoulder to lean on, his arm about her, she felt safe.

'And…' he insisted, refusing to let her off the hook.

He really wanted to know what she'd done next, did he? Well, that would speed reality along very nicely and maybe that was a good thing. Illusions were made to be shattered, so it was best to get it over with. The sooner the better.

'You're absolutely right,' she said. 'There's always an "and".'

'You're stalling.'

'Am I?'

Who wouldn't?

'And so I went looking for someone who would,' she said. 'Just one more poor little rich girl looking for someone who'd hold her and tell her that he loved her. Totally pathetic.'

Just how dumb could a girl get?

'You were what? Eighteen?' he guessed. 'I don't suppose you found it difficult.'

'No. It wasn't finding someone that was difficult. There were someones positively lining up to help me out. Finding

them wasn't the problem. Keeping them was something else.'
Looking back with the crystal clear vision of hindsight, it was
easy to see why. 'Needy, clinging women desperate for love
frighten men to death.'

'We're a pitiful bunch.'

She shook her head. 'It wasn't their fault. They were young,
looking for some light-hearted fun. Sex without strings.'

Something she hadn't understood at the time. And when,
finally, it had been made clear to her, it had broken her.

'I think you're being a little harsh on yourself.'

'Am I?' She heard the longing in her voice and dismissed
it. 'I don't think so.'

'There's no such thing as sex without strings, especially
for women.'

'You're referring to that old thing about men giving love
for sex, women giving sex for love, no doubt.'

'I'm not sure anything as complex as the relationship
between a man and woman can ever be reduced to a sound
bite,' he said.

'It can when you've just taken your finals and the world
beckons. No young man with the world at his feet wants to
be saddled with a baby.'

'You were pregnant?' That stopped him. She'd known it
would.

'My last throw of the dice. I thought if I had his baby a man
wouldn't ever be able to leave me. Stupid. Unfair. Irrespon-
sible beyond belief.'

'People do crazy things when they're unhappy,' he said.

'No excuses, Nick. Using a child...' She shrugged. 'Of
course he insisted I terminate the pregnancy and, well, I've
already told you that I'd have done anything...'

'Where is this child now?'

'You're assuming I didn't go ahead with it.' How generous of him. How undeserved…

'Are you saying you did?'

They were lying quite still but when, beside her, Nick Jago stopped breathing, it felt as if the world had stopped.

'My punishment,' Manda said, at last, 'is not knowing. I was standing at the kerb, looking across the road to the clinic, when I collapsed in agony in front of a car and matters were taken out of my hands.'

And with that everything started again. His breathing, her heart…

'You lost the baby?'

'Not because of the accident. The driver saved my life twice over that day. First stopping his car. Then realising that there was something seriously wrong and calling an ambulance.'

'You were in that much pain? Was it an ectopic pregnancy?'

She nodded. 'By the time Ivo made it back from wherever he was, I was home and it was over. A minor traffic accident. Nothing to make a fuss over.'

'You never told him? You lost your baby and you never told him?'

'He already had the world on his shoulders. He didn't need me as well. And I was so ashamed…'

'You didn't do anything.'

'I thought about it, Jago. I was so desperate…'

He muttered something beneath his breath, then said, 'And this man who could demand such a thing? Where was he when all this was happening?'

'Keeping his fingers crossed that I'd go through with it?' she offered. Then, with a shrug, 'No, that's unfair. He came rushing to the hospital to make sure I was okay, but I couldn't bear to look at him any more. Couldn't bear to see his relief. Face what I'd done.'

'You hadn't done anything,' Jago said, reaching for her, taking her into his arms in that eternal gesture of comfort.

Did he think she would cry again? Before, her tears had been of relief. A normal, human reaction. But this was different. She had no more tears to cry for herself…

'You would never have gone through with it,' he said, holding her close. And he kept on saying it. Telling her that it was not her fault, that she shouldn't blame herself. Saying over and over, that she would not have rejected her own baby.

This was the absolution she'd dreamed of. And why she'd never told anyone.

She didn't deserve such comfort. It had been no one's fault but her own that she'd been pregnant. It was her burden. Her loss. And she pulled away.

'How did you guess it was ectopic?' she asked. How many men knew what an ectopic pregnancy was, without it being explained in words of one syllable?

'My grandfather was a doctor, wanted me to follow in his footsteps and maybe I would have, if I hadn't been taken to Egypt at an early age…' For a moment he drifted off somewhere else, to a memory of his own. Happier times with his family, no doubt. Then, shaking it off, he said, 'I remember him talking about a patient of his who'd nearly died. Describing the symptoms. He said the pain was indescribable.'

It wasn't the pain that she remembered. It was the emptiness afterwards, the lack of feeling that never ceased…

'What happened to you, Miranda? Afterwards.'

'The next logical step, I suppose. My parents, my boyfriend, even my baby had rejected me. All that was left was to reject myself so I stopped eating.' Then, because she didn't want to think about that, because she wanted to hear about Egypt and Jago as an impressionable boy, however unlikely that seemed, she said, 'What about you?'

'Manda…'

'No. Enough about me. I want to hear about you,' she insisted, telling herself that his use of the diminutive had been nothing more than a slip. It meant nothing…

'In Egypt?' he asked.

Yes… No… Egypt was a distraction and she refused to be distracted.

'When you walked away from your family,' she said.

She felt the movement of muscle, more jerk than shrug, as if she'd taken him unawares. The slight catch in his breathing as if he'd jolted some pain into life. Physical? Or deeper?

Then, realising that she was transferring her own mental pain on to him, that it had to be physical, she sat up. 'You *are* hurt!'

'It's nothing. Lie back.' And, when she hesitated, 'Honestly. Just a pulled muscle. It needs warmth and you make a most acceptable hot-water bottle.'

'Would that be "Dr" Jago talking?'

'I don't think you need to be a doctor to know that.'

'I guess not.' And, since warmth was all she had to offer, she eased gently back against him, taking care not to jar his shoulder.

'Is that okay?'

'Fine,' he said, tightening his arm around her waist so that she felt as if she was a perfect fit against him.

Too perfect.

'So?' she said, returning to her question, determined not to get caught, dragged down by the sexual undertow of their closeness, a totally unexpected—totally unwanted—off limits desire that was nothing more than a response to fear.

She didn't want to like Nick Jago, let alone care about him.

Not easy when a man had saved your life. When his kiss had first warmed her, then heated her to the bone.

And the last thing she wanted was his pity.

CHAPTER NINE

'TELL me about your life,' she pressed. 'Away from here. Are you, or have you ever been, married?' she asked, using the interrogatory technique of the immigration form. Turning the question into something of a joke. 'How about children?'

Jago didn't make the mistake of shrugging a second time, just said, 'No, no and none.'

'None that you know of,' she quipped.

'None, full stop. I'm not that careless.'

'I'm sorry…'

'It's okay. It's one of those hideous things that men say, isn't it? As if it makes them look big.'

'Some men,' she agreed. Then, before she could stop herself, 'What about long-term relationships?'

She was making too much of it, she knew. It didn't matter. Tomorrow, please God, they'd be out of here and would have no reason to ever see one another again.

They'd step back into their own lives and be desperate to forget that, locked in the darkness, they'd shared the darkest secrets of their souls with a stranger.

'What about the woman who's been telling the world that this…' she made a small gesture that took in their unseen sur-roundings '…was all her own work?'

'Fliss? I was under the apparently mistaken impression that she came under the sex-without-strings heading. She was, allegedly, a postgraduate archaeology student and when she turned up on site looking for work experience I was glad to have another pair of hands. My mistake. I should have made an effort to check her credentials.'

'As opposed to her "credentials",' Manda said, unable to help herself from teasing him a little. 'Which, let's face it, no one could fail to miss.'

'You've got me.' He laughed, taking no offence. 'Shallow as a puddle and clearly getting no more than I deserve.'

'Which is?'

'Being made to look a fool? Although maybe the gods have had the last laugh after all,' he said, no longer amused. 'The temples, as a tourist attraction, which was the entire point of that scurrilous piece of garbage she and the Tourism Minister concocted between them, would seem to be dead in the water. And what does my reputation matter? The suffering caused by this earthquake is far more important.'

He took the bottle of brandy from her bag and offered it to her.

'No. Thanks.'

'Just take a mouthful to wash the dust out of your mouth,' he suggested, 'then maybe it really would be a good idea to try and get some sleep.'

She eased forward, took the bottle, gasping as a little of the hot liquor slid down her throat, for a moment totally unable to speak.

'Good grief,' she managed finally. 'Do people actually drink this stuff?'

'Only the desperate,' he admitted.

'It would be quicker—and kinder—to shoot yourself.

Here,' she said, passing it back to him. 'Can you pass me my bag?'

He handed it to her, then eased himself carefully into a sitting position.

He *was* in pain.

Had he just pulled a muscle? Or had he torn something in that long, desperate moment when he'd hung on to her? When he'd helped her over the top to safety.

She didn't ask, knew he'd deny it anyway. Instead, she dug out the nearly empty pack of wipes from the soggy interior of her bag. Then, having used one to wipe the worst of the dust from her face and hands, she took another and, lifting the big capable hand that had held her, had hung on as the earth shook beneath them, she began, very gently, to wipe it clean.

Jago stiffened at the first touch of the cool, damp cloth on his thumb.

'Manda...'

Not a slip, then...

'Shh...' she said. 'Let me do this.'

Even through the cloth, she could feel a callus along the inner edge of his thumb that she knew would be a fit for the small trowel he'd found. The result of years of carefully sifting through the layers of the past.

Pieces of bone, pottery, the occasional button or scrap of leather that had been preserved by some freak chance of nature.

Objects without emotional context. Small pieces of distant lives that wouldn't break your heart.

'Don't worry, I've learned my lesson. I won't throw myself on you,' she said as she concentrated on each of his fingers in turn. 'I haven't done that in years.'

'No? Just my bad luck.' Then, as if realising that he'd said something crass, 'So what do you do with yourself? Now you've given up on men?'

'I work. Very hard. I used to work for Ivo, but these days I'm a partner in the television production company that I set up with my sister-in-law,' she said, smoothing the cloth over his broad palm. 'I'm the organiser. I co-ordinate the research, find the people, the places. Keep things running smoothly behind the scenes while Belle does the touchy-feely stuff in front of the camera.'

'Maybe you should change places,' he said as, having finished one hand, she began on the other.

She looked up.

'You're doing just fine with the touchy-feely stuff,' he assured her.

'Oh. No. This is…' Then, pulling herself together, 'Actually, since we recently won an award for our first documentary, I think I'll leave things just the way they are.'

'What was it about?'

'Not handbags,' she said. 'Or shoes.'

'I didn't imagine for a minute it was.'

'I'm sorry.'

'No. It's my fault for making uncalled-for comments on your handbag choices. Tell me about it.'

'It was all tied up with one of Belle's pet causes.' He waited. 'Street kids…'

'The unwanted. You're sure this was your sister-in-law's pet cause?'

He was too damn quick…

'She and her sister spent some time on the streets when they were children. Their stories put my pathetic whining in its place, I can tell you,' she said quickly. 'How's your head, Jago?'

'Still there last time I looked, Miranda.'

'Your sense of humour is still intact, at least. Let me see,' she said, cupping his face in her hands so that she could check it out for herself.

It had been so long since she'd touched a man's hand, his face in this way. His lean jaw was long past the five o'clock stubble phase and she had to restrain herself from the sensuous pleasure of rubbing her palms against it. Instead, she pushed back his hair, searching out the injury on his forehead.

He'd really taken quite a crack, she discovered, remembering uncomfortably how she'd taunted him about that.

'I'd better clean that up,' she said, taking the last wipe from the pack.

'I can—'

'Tut…' she said, slapping away his hand as he tried to take it from her.

'I can do it myself,' he persisted. 'But why would I when I have a beautiful woman to tend me?'

She stopped what she was doing.

The crack on his head must have jarred his brains loose, he decided. Despite all evidence to the contrary, he wasn't given to living dangerously, at least not where women were concerned.

Keeping it light, keeping his distance just about summed up his attitude to the entire sex, but ever since he'd woken to the sound of Miranda Grenville screaming in the dark it was as if he'd been walking on a high wire. Carelessly.

Maybe cheating death gave you the kind of reckless edge that had you saying the most outrageous things to a woman who was quite capable of responding with painful precision. A woman who, like a well-known brand of chocolate, kept her soft and vulnerable centre hidden beneath a hard, protective sugar shell.

'You have no idea what I look like,' she said crisply as she leaned into him, continued her careful cleaning of the abrasion. Enveloping him in her warm female scent.

Would her shell melt against the tongue, too? Dissolve into silky sweetness…

'I know enough,' he said, taking advantage of the fact that she had her own hands full to run the pad of his thumb across her forehead, down the length of her nose, across a well defined cheekbone. Definitely his brains had been shaken loose. 'I know that you've got good bones. A strong face.'

'A big nose, you mean,' she said as, job done, she leaned back. 'How does that feel now?'

That she was too far away.

'You missed a bit just here,' he said, taking her hand and guiding it an inch or two to the right. Then to his temple. 'And there.'

'Really?' She slid her fingers across his skin. 'I can't feel anything. Maybe I should have the light.'

'We should save the battery,' he said. 'You're doing just fine. So, where was I? Oh, yes, your nose. Is it big? I'd have said interesting…'

'You are full of it, Nick Jago.'

'Brimful,' he admitted, beginning to enjoy himself. 'Your hair is straight. It's very dark and cut at chin-length.'

'How do you know my hair is dark?' She stopped dabbing at his imaginary injuries… 'Did you take a sneaky photograph of me?'

'As a souvenir of a special day, you mean?' It hadn't occurred to him down in the blackness of the temple when his entire focus had been on getting them out of there. Almost his entire focus. Miranda Grenville had a way of making you take notice of her. 'Maybe I should do it now,' he suggested.

'I don't think so.' She moved instinctively to protect the

phone tucked away in her breast pocket. 'Who'd want a reminder of this to stick on the mantelpiece?' She shivered. 'Who would need one? Besides, as you said, we need to conserve what's left of the battery.'

His mistake.

'I was talking about the light, not the cellphone but I take your point. But, to get back to your question, I know your hair is dark because if it had been fair then the light, feeble though it was, would have reflected off it.'

'Mmm… Well, Mr Smarty Pants, you've got dark hair, too. It's definitely not straight and it needs cutting. I saw that much when you struck your one and only match.' Then, 'Oh, and you're left-handed.'

'How on earth do you know that?' he demanded.

'There's a callus on your thumb. Here.' She rubbed the tender tip of her own thumb against the ridge of hard skin. 'This is the hand you use first. The one you reached out to me when I couldn't make it across that last gap.' She lifted it in both of hers and said, 'This is the hand with which you held me safe.'

It was the hand with which he'd held her when she'd cried out to him to let her fall because she was not worth dying for. Because once, young, alone, in despair and on the point of a breakdown, she'd considered terminating a pregnancy?

Had she been punishing herself for that ever since?

'You are worth it, Manda,' he said, his voice catching in his throat. Then, 'No, I hate that. You deserve better than some childish pet name. You are an amazing woman, Miranda. A survivor. And, whatever it is you want, you are worth it.'

'Thank you…' Her words were little more than a whisper and, in the darkness, he felt the brush of silky hair against his wrist, then soft lips, the touch of warm breath against his knuckles. A kiss. No, more than a kiss, a salute, and something that had lain undisturbed inside him for aeons contracted, or expanded, he couldn't have said which. Only that her touch had moved him beyond words.

It was Miranda who shattered the moment, removing her hands from his, putting clear air between them. Shattered the silence, rescuing them both from a moment in which he might have said, done, anything.

'Actually, I'm not the only one around here with an interesting nose,' she said. Her voice was too bright, her attempt at a laugh forced. 'Yours has been broken at some time. How did that happen?' Then, archly, deliberately breaking the spell of that brief intimacy, 'Or, more interestingly, who did it to you?'

'You saw all that in the flare of a match?' he asked.

'You were looking at your temple. I was looking at the bad-tempered drunk I was unfortunate to have been trapped with.'

'I was not drunk,' he protested, belatedly grabbing for the lifeline she'd flung him. Stepping back from a brink far more dangerous than the dark opening that yawned a few feet away from them.

She shook her head, then, perhaps thinking that because he couldn't see, he didn't know what she'd done—and how had he known?—she said, 'I know that now, but for a while back there you didn't seem too sure.'

'A crack on the head will do that to you.'

'Concussion?'

'I hope not. The treatment is rest and plenty of fluids.'

'Thus speaks the voice of experience?'

'Well, you know how it is.'

'Er, no, actually, I don't. I suspect it's a boy thing.' Then, presumably because there really wasn't anything else to say about that, 'And, actually, no, I didn't see your nose. I felt it.'

'Yes…'

That was it. How he'd known she'd shaken her head. He could *feel* the smallest movement that she made. Without sight, every little sound, every disturbance in the air was heightened beyond imagining and his brain was somehow able to translate them into a picture. Just as every tiny nuance in her voice was amplified so that he could not only hear what she was saying, he could also hear what she was not.

The air moved and he saw the quick shake of her head, the slide of glossy, sharply cut hair. He touched her face and saw a peaches and cream complexion. Kissed her and—

'I felt it when I cleaned the dust from your face,' she said, her rising inflexion replying to some uncertainty that she'd picked up in his voice. It was a two-way thing then, and he wondered what image came into her mind when he moved, spoke. When she touched him…

'As noses go,' he said, 'I have to admit that it's hard to miss.'

'Oh, it's not that bad. Just a little battered. How did it happen?'

She was back in control now, her voice level, with no little emotional yips to betray her. She'd clearly trained herself to disguise her feelings. How long had it taken, he wondered.

How long before it had become part of her?

How long had it taken him?

'At school,' he said. 'It was at a rugby match. I charged down a ball that was on the point of leaving another boy's boot.'

'Ouch.'

'I was feeling no pain, believe me,' he said, remembering the moment, even so many years later, with complete satisfaction. 'I'd stopped an almost certain last-minute drop goal that would have stolen the match. I don't think I'd have noticed a broken leg, let alone a flattened nose. I was just mad that I had to go to A and E instead of going out with…'

He stopped, his pleasure at the memory tripping him over another, spilling his own emotional baggage.

'Out with?' she prompted, then, when he didn't respond, 'It was your father, wasn't it? He'd come to see you play.'

'Yes…'

How could that one small word have so many shades? he wondered. In the last few moments it had been a revelation, a question, reassurance and now an acknowledgement of a truth that he could barely admit. Because she was right. His father had been there. Even with an election looming, he'd taken time out of a packed schedule to be with him that day.

'Yes,' he repeated. 'My father had come to see the match.'

'Good photo op, was it?' she asked dismissively. 'Senior politician with his son, the blood-spattered hero of the sports field. I bet it looked terrific in the papers the next day.'

'No!' he responded angrily. That touch of derision in her voice had him leaping to his father's defence. How dared she…?

'No?' she repeated, but this time the ironic inflection didn't fool him.

'There was no photograph,' he said, his voice flat, giving her nothing.

'No photograph? But surely you said that was all it ever was?'

She was pure butter-wouldn't-melt-in-her-mouth innocence, but he knew that it had been a deliberate trip-up. That she'd heard something in his voice—his own emotional yip—and had set out to prove something.

'So—what?' she persisted, refusing to let him off her clever little hook. 'He turned up just to see his son play for his school like any other proud father? No agenda? No photo opportunity?'

She did that thing with her fingers—making quotation marks—and he grabbed at her hands to make her stop.

'You are a witch, Miranda Grenville.'

'I've been called worse,' she replied, so softly that her voice wrapped itself around him.

'I can believe it.' Then, her hands still in his, he said, 'It was my birthday that week. My eighteenth. Dad came down from London to watch the match before taking me out to dinner.'

'You missed your birthday dinner?'

'Actually, it was okay,' he said. 'We sat in A and E, eating sandwiches out of a machine, surrounded by the walking wounded, a couple of drunks, while we waited for someone to fix me up. Give me a shot.'

'Waited? Are you telling me that as the son of a Government minister you didn't get instant attention?' she said, still mocking him, but gently now.

'The doctors were busy with more serious stuff. It didn't matter. We talked about what I was going to do on my gap year. About the election. It wasn't often I got him to myself like that.'

'So the evening wasn't a total wash-out.'

'Not a wash-out on any level,' he admitted. It had been the last time they'd been together like that. His father had been given a high-powered cabinet job after the election. He'd gone to university.

Manda knelt back on her heels, her hands gripped with painful tightness as Nick, seemingly unaware of her, relived a precious evening spent with his father. Did he, she wondered, realise how lucky he was?

She yearned for just one memory like that.

One day when her mother or father had taken time out of their busy lives to come and see her at school, take her out for tea. For her birthday to have been more than a date in a secretary's diary.

'I suppose now you're going to tell me that I should remember all the good bits, forget the rest,' he said, breaking into her own dark thoughts.

'I wouldn't dream of suggesting any such thing,' she said.

'Don't be so modest, Miranda. We both know that you would.'

'Then we'd both be wrong,' she said vehemently. 'I'd tell you to remember all of it. Every little thing. The good, the bad, the totally average and be grateful for every single moment.' She caught herself. Shrugged awkwardly. 'Sorry. It's none of my business.'

The stone was hurting her knees and she shifted to a sitting position.

'Here. Lean back against me, you'll be more comfortable.' Then, his arm around her, he said, 'Tell me one of your memories, Miranda. Your first day at school. Was that good? Bad? Totally average?'

'Not great. All the other new girls had been brought along by their mothers. Mine was away somewhere.' She had always been away. 'Let's see… September? Shooting in Scotland, probably. Anyway, I told whichever unhappy creature was my nanny at the time to take me home since obviously it had to be a mother who delivered me to school.'

'Did she?'

'What do you think? The poor woman couldn't wait to be shot of me and I was handed over kicking and screaming. No reprieve. A first impression that I strived to live down to. Can you remember your first day?'

'I wish I couldn't. My mother cried. I was so embarrassed that I wouldn't let her take me nearer than the end of the road after that.'

'Oh, poor woman!'

'What about me? I had to live with the shame.'

'What horrible little brats we both were.'

'We were five years old. We were supposed to be horrible little brats.'

'I suppose.'

'Tell me about your first kiss,' he said.

She sighed. 'We're doing all the horrible stuff first, are we?'

'Was it horrible?'

'I was fourteen. That dreadful age when you're pretending to be grown up but you're not. When kissing is a competitive sport, something to be dissected in detail with your friends afterwards and points awarded for technical merit, artistic style and endurance. Mine was with a boy called Jonathan Powell, all clashing teeth and acne. Of course, when we compared notes afterwards I lied through my back teeth. You?'

'Thirteen. Her name was Lucy… Something. I think she must have been practising because I had a really good time.'

'Not just a brat, but a precocious brat and, before you even think of taking this to the next logical step,' she warned, 'forget it.'

'Okay. You choose. Tell me something that happened to you. Something that's stayed with you.'

'My very own heart-warming moment?' she replied, mocking herself.

'I don't know. Have you got a heart to be warmed?'

'Bastard,' she said, but laughing now.

She'd never talked like this to a man. It was as if, sheared of all expectations, freed by the darkness, they could be totally honest with one another. Could say anything.

'And now you've got that off your chest?' he prompted.

'Okay. A memory. Let's see.'

She dredged her mind for something that would satisfy

him—something big—and, without warning, she was back on the streets, scouting locations for the documentary. 'At the beginning of the year I took my colleague Daisy on a worldwide recce to find locations where we could film our documentary.'

'The one about street kids.'

'Right. We'd been all over. It was all done and dusted and we were on our way home from the airport when Daisy told the taxi driver to stop—wait for us—and dragged me down a side alley.'

She could still see it. Smell it.

'We were in one of the richest countries in the world, metres from the kind of stores where women like me buy handbags that cost four figures, restaurants where we toy with expensive food that we're afraid to eat in case we put on a pound or two. And there was this kid, a little girl, Rosie, digging around in a dumpster for food that had been thrown away.'

He let slip the same word that had dropped from her lips. Shock, horror…

'I'd known such things happened,' she said. She shook her head, for a moment unable to say another word. 'I'd known, but blocked it out. To see it with my own eyes…'

'It isn't your fault.'

'Isn't it? Isn't it the fault of everyone who looks the other way? Blocks it out?' Even now, her throat tightened as she remembered the shock of it. The horror. 'I felt so helpless. It was freezing cold and I wanted to pick her up, carry her away, wash her, feed her, make her safe, but Daisy…' she swallowed as she remembered '…Daisy just walked over and joined in, helping her look for the best stuff. It was the most horrible thing I'd ever seen in my life but she'd been there, lived it. Knew how to connect with her. And it was that child's story that touched people, had the country in an uproar, demanding that something be done. Her thin, grubby, defiant little face on the cover of magazines, looking out of the screen, that won us our award.'

'And you feel guilty about that?'

'Wouldn't you? Where was she when I was picking it up at a ritzy awards ceremony decked out in a designer dress?'

'What were you going to do, Miranda? Take in every kid that you saw on the street? Your job was to focus on what was out there, raise public awareness. You helped all those kids, not just one.' Then, when she didn't say anything, 'What did happen to her? Do you know?'

She shook her head. 'As you can imagine, thousands of couples wanted to give her a home. Adopt her.'

'But not you?'

'No,' she said, trying to keep her voice steady. 'Not me.' Then, 'Have you any idea how tough it is to take in a feral child? To make her believe that you'll never let her down, no matter what she does. Because she'll test you...'

She faltered and Jago let go of one of her hands and wiped a thumb over her cheek. It came away wet, just as he'd known it would.

'Something that you'd know all about, right?' He didn't need or wait for an answer, but pulled her into his arms and held her. 'Tough as marshmallow.'

She dug an elbow in his ribs.

'Ouch!'

'Well, what do you expect?' she demanded through a sniffle. 'Marshmallow! I don't think so!'

'No? Maybe not,' he said, remembering his earlier thought that she was like those sugar-coated, melt in your mouth chocolates. All hard shell on the outside... 'Turkish Delight?' he offered, tormenting her to block out the image.

'How about seaside rock?'

'No way.' His head and shoulder hurt when he laughed, but the very idea of her as a stick of bright pink mint-flavoured candy with her name printed all the way through was so outrageous that he couldn't help himself. 'I'll bet the majority of your wardrobe is black.'

She didn't deny it, but countered with, 'Liquorice. I'll settle for liquorice. That's black. But it has to have been in the fridge.'

'Now you're talking,' he said and his stomach approved noisily too. 'Maybe we should stop talking about food.'

'I've still got three mints left.' She turned her head to look up at him. 'They're yours if you want them.'

'With my three that makes a feast, but let's save them for breakfast.' Then, because he hadn't eaten since early the previous morning and needed a distraction, 'When we get out of here, you should go and find her. That little girl.'

'It wouldn't be fair, Nick.'

'You've thought about it, then?'

She didn't deny it, but shook her head anyway. 'It'll be tough enough for her to move on, for her new parents, without me turning up and bringing it all back.'

'Maybe you could keep an eye on her from a distance. It would put your mind at rest. And you'll be there in case she ever needs a fairy godmother.'

'Kids don't need fairy godmothers, Nick. They need real mothers who are there for them every day, rain or shine, doing the boring stuff. Parents who earn love the hard way every day of their lives.'

He knew she was right. Knew she was talking about more than a little girl whose life she'd changed.

'You think I was hard on my parents, don't you?'

'Yes. No… I don't know.' She drew in a deep breath. 'I don't know anything, Nick. I'm just imagining what would happen if one of them was sick. If your mother needed you. Your father wanted to make some kind of peace…' He thought she'd finished, but then, very quietly, she said, 'Suppose you'd died here without ever having told them how much you love them—'

'I don't!'

'Of course you do, Nick. It only hurts if you love someone.'

Her words seemed to echo around the chamber, filling the space, filling his head, until, almost in desperation he said, 'We're not going to die. Not today.'

CHAPTER TEN

MIRANDA drew a breath and for a moment he thought she wasn't going to let it drop. Instead, with a little shake of her head, she said, 'Is it still today? It seems a lifetime since I walked up that path, wishing I was somewhere else.'

'You should be careful what you wish for.'

'Thanks,' she said, fishing the phone from her pocket and turning it on to check the time. 'I'll remember that for next time.' Then, with a sigh of relief, 'No, it's tomorrow. Just. How long before it's going to be light?'

He glanced at the screen. 'A few hours yet.' He felt her shiver but not with cold. Shock, hunger and thirst were doubtless taking their toll on her reserves. 'Why don't you check your messages?' he suggested in an attempt to reconnect her to reality, the outside world.

'The battery…'

'We're not going anywhere until daylight,' he assured her, overriding any protest. 'Read them. Text back. Tell them what you're feeling.'

'I don't think so! Besides, what's the point if there's no signal?' Then, catching his meaning, 'Oh. I see. You're suggesting I send them a last message. Something for them to find if we don't make it?'

Did he mean that? Maybe…

At least she had someone to leave a message for.

'We're going to make it,' he said with more conviction than he actually felt. Who knew what daylight would reveal? They might still have to climb their way out and they were weaker now and he'd be operating pretty much one-handed. He wouldn't be able to catch her a second time. 'You'll be seeing them all before you know it, but sending a message will make you feel better.'

'You think? And what about you, Nick?'

'What about me?'

'Is there anyone you want to leave a last message for? What will make you feel better?'

He knew what she was asking him. Telling him. To leave a message for his parents. He could see how she must find it difficult to understand how he could have walked away, how destroyed he'd felt. But they had been his world. They'd brought him up to believe in the cardinal virtues. Integrity, truth. He'd believed in *them*. He'd believed in a lie…

'I'll take another of those kisses, if you've got one to spare,' he said in an attempt to stop her from pursuing that thought.

Manda heard what she was supposed to hear—a careless, throwaway remark, pitched perfectly to provoke her into giving him another poke in the ribs, to distract her.

But she heard more.

Somewhere, hidden beneath the banter, she caught an edge of something she recognised.

Nick Jago, with no other way to push back the darkness, to distract her from her fear, her hunger, had shared his story. To help her feel a little less alone, he'd exposed a hurt that went so deep he'd cut himself off from his world, even to the point of changing his name.

She understood that kind of pain. How it was tied up with

everything you were. Knew how, in order to keep it hidden, you had to wear a mask every day of your life until it became so much a part of you that even those closest to you believed that was who you were.

Until, eventually, you believed it yourself and, unless someone took a risk to save you, took a step into their own darkest place to release a lifetime of unwanted, unused love and give all they had, you would shrivel up until something vital inside you died.

Nick Jago had saved her from certain death. What would it take to save him from the living death to which he'd condemned himself?

He'd answered her question, but could it really be that simple?

'A kiss?' she repeated.

The air was still and, above them, in the small patch of sky that was visible, Venus shone like a beacon of hope.

'Would that be a kissing-it-better kiss?' she asked, softly, lightly, matching his careless tone. 'Or are we talking about a make-the-world-go-away kiss?'

Jago had been deliberately provoking. He'd counted on that to divert her, keep her from the saying the words he did not want to hear, to force him to face a situation that he had blanked from his mind.

He'd anticipated a swift response too. The seemingly endless pause between presumption and response was unexpected, a touch unnerving.

But then her teasing tone as, finally, she'd repeated, 'A kiss?' had reassured him and, braced for whatever she chose to visit upon him, the butterfly touch of her fingers on his cheek, the caress of her thumb over his lips as she took him at his word, asked him what he truly wanted, warned him that this was anything but a reprieve.

He'd barely drawn breath, determined to apologise, reassure her that he'd been joking—put a stop to something that had, in the time it had taken to say it, spun out of control—before her lips touched his with a pressure so soft that he could almost have imagined it.

And then breathing seemed an irrelevance as the slow, penetrating warmth of it heated his lips, seeped into his veins, spread through his body like liquid silk until he was feeling no pain.

It was a kiss of almost unbearable sweetness that gave and gave, growing in intensity while the tips of her fingers slid down his neck, seeking out the pulse point beneath his jaw. And her touch, when she found it, sent a current of pure energy through him, as if she was somehow concentrating her entire being into that one spot.

It was as if, for years, his entire body had been somehow lying dormant, barely ticking over, waiting for this. Waiting for Miranda Grenville to come down into the dark to kiss him into life. Wake him with a touch.

Only her feather-light fingertips, her breath, her lips, touched him, seeking out the hollows, the sensitive places beneath his chin, his throat, stirring not just his body, but something deeper.

She took endless time, her lips, her tongue, lingering as she made her way down the hard line of his breastbone, slipping shirt buttons as she moved lower, her silky hair brushing against his chest as she laid it bare to the chill night air.

For a moment she lay her hand over his heart and it, too, leapt to her touch. Then it was not her hand, but her mouth against his breast, breathing her warmth, her life into the cold, angry core that had for so long masqueraded as his heart. It was an almost unbearably sweet agony, like that of a numb limb coming painfully to life.

'Miranda…'

He gasped her name out but whether he wanted her to revive him or leave him in the safety of the cold and dark place where there was no feeling he could not have said.

'Nick?' Jago was aware that Manda was speaking to him, that there was an edge of concern to her voice. 'Are you okay?'

Was he? He was feeling a touch light-headed. Not particularly surprising under the circumstances. That hadn't been a mere kissing-it-better kiss…

'Nick!' she repeated more urgently.

'Fine,' he murmured. 'More than fine.' He hooked his arm around her. 'Lie down,' he said, pulling her up to lie against him, her hair against his cheek. 'Try and get some sleep.'

Manda lay with her cheek against Nick Jago's chest, his arm pinning her down so that she couldn't move without disturbing him. And he seemed to have drifted off almost as soon as he'd said the word.

If it was sleep.

For a minute back there she'd thought he'd drifted out of consciousness. But his heartbeat was steady beneath her ear and his breathing seemed okay…

She closed her eyes. Tried not to think of the aches and pains that she'd temporarily managed to block out, but now she'd stopped concentrating on Nick had returned with a vengeance.

The fact that she was hungry. Thirsty. She hadn't had anything to drink other than a few sips of water since lunch. A lunch she'd done little more than toy with. Sleep, if she could manage it, would be a great idea.

She closed her eyes, concentrating on the slow, steady beat of Nick's heartbeat until, gradually, it began to lull her.

* * *

It was the light that woke her. Searingly bright against her lids, she moved instinctively to escape it, for a moment completely disorientated. Hurting everywhere. Her neck stiff.

She lifted her head to ease the ache and realised that she was lying against the supine figure of a man.

Nick Jago…

She sat up with a gasp as it all came back with a rush. Tried to speak, but her mouth was dry, her lips cracked and it took a couple of goes before she could manage his name.

'Nick? Wake up! It's morning!'

Manda disentangled herself, scrambling quickly to her feet, forgetting all aches and pains in her eagerness to explore this promise of a way out.

Then, when he didn't respond, she looked back.

'Jago?' He was drowsy, slow to stir. Slow to stifle a groan. 'Are you okay?' she asked, remembering his hurt shoulder. That he'd had a bang on the head.

'Barely,' he muttered. 'There are alarm clocks that use fewer decibels than you. Your wake-up technique could do with a little polishing, Miranda.'

'I just haven't been putting in the practise,' she said, glancing back.

The sun, barely over the horizon, had found a chink in the shattered walls and for a moment it was concentrated on their corner of the dark interior and she caught her first real glimpse of the man with whom she'd spent the long night. Whose hand had brought her from the depths. Whose arm had held her safe.

His face was craggy rather than handsome, not helped by the fact that he needed a shave. His nose was, as they'd already discussed, interesting. His chin, stubborn. His eyes, she saw, in the moment before he blinked and lifted a hand to shade them from the light, were a fine grey. As for his mouth…

His mouth, she thought, looked exactly the way it had felt as she'd traced it with her thumb. The way it had felt when he'd kissed her. Tender, determined, sensuous. As if it had been a long time since he'd smiled.

He leaned his head back against the wall and, suddenly concerned, she said, 'Are you really okay?'

'I'd be better if you sat down instead of flirting with that big empty space out there in the dark.'

She glanced at the wall, with its tantalising promise of light, then dropped to her knees and pushed his hair back from his forehead to check his injury. There was a brutal graze, bruising, a slight swelling. Then, as the rising sun moved, the light suddenly disappeared, plunging them back into deep shadow.

'I think you'll live,' she said, dropping her hand.

'I know I will,' he replied softly. 'You gave me the kiss of life.'

'Did I? When we get out of here…'

'When we get out of here you'll find the child you filmed on the streets. And I'll get in touch with my parents. Is that a deal?'

'It's a deal,' she said.

And, as if to seal their pact, he reached out and touched her lips with the edge of his thumb. 'Hello, Miranda Grenville.'

'Hello, Nick Jago.'

'No!'

'What? I'm sorry…'

'When someone has saved your life they have the right to know who you really are.' There was a pause, during which she swallowed desperately. 'I was born Nicholas Alexander Jackson—the good, solid English name that my grandfather chose for himself within weeks of arriving in England.'

Jackson… 'But…' She'd actually met his father at some reception or other. Ivo had introduced him, told her afterwards that he and his wife worked quietly these days, without any public fanfare, to raise funds for a charity that helped runaways. Used their own wealth, inherited from the same grandfather who'd gone on to found a giant food conglomerate…

'What?'

She shook her head. Telling him that his father had changed would be pointless. He had to be open to the possibility before he could hear it. See for himself. And he'd made that commitment. It was enough.

'Nothing. Just, thank you for telling me. Nick,' she added.

He drew in a deep breath and it was her turn to say, 'What?'

'It's just been a very long time since anyone's called me that.' Then, briskly, 'Right. So, what do you say? Shall we get out of here?'

'Yes. Please.'

Jago made it to his feet. Last night he'd thought he'd never make it out of here, but now, with even the small amount of light filtering through the broken walls, seeping down the shaft, anything seemed possible.

He looked around. He'd hoped for a way out through the original entrance but, even if it hadn't been completely blocked by falling masonry, it was on the far side of the gaping chasm where the great eagle below had broken away. But above them was the promise of a small patch of sky and he stood up to take a better look.

'Careful,' he said, reaching back to offer a steadying hand as Miranda rose beside him. 'I don't want to lose you now.' And then, as she took it, he turned back.

With the narrow beam of sunlight behind her, her face in shadow, all he'd seen of her had been the halo effect as it had lit up hair that was no longer sleek but suffering from the effects of twenty-four hours without the benefit of a comb.

Thick, dark, tousled.

He'd guessed that she was tall, but not quite how tall. No more than half a head shorter than himself. Tall, slender but with a steel core of strength about her. Well, he knew that. He'd experienced that. As a girl she might have broken down under the twin assaults of rejection and guilt, but this woman had come through a living nightmare with courage, humour, compassion.

Now, the light from above shimmered through the haze of dust motes and he could see that her black halo of hair was veiled with stone dust. There were streaks of dirt, like warpaint, decorating her cheek, her neck.

She did not have the instant, softer sensual attraction of a woman like Fliss. She had a different kind of beauty—taut, tempered in the fire—and she'd still be beautiful even when she was ninety.

She was beautiful now.

'What?' she asked, catching him staring, lifting her hand to her cheek, suddenly self-conscious of how she must look and that was when he saw her hands.

They were small, the fingers long, slender, elegant, well cared for—the remains of polish still clung to what was left of her nails—were a mess. The skin torn, knuckles bruised and broken.

She saw where he was looking and, mistaking his reaction, she spread her hand, regarding it with distaste. 'My manicurist is going to have a fit when she sees this,' she said, taking a step back to that woman who'd roused him with her scream, God alone knew how many hours ago.

Putting the mask back in place before she returned to the outside world.

'Don't!' he said. He was not a man given to fanciful

gestures, but he would not let her slide back into that dark place any more than he would have left her to fall and he reached for her hand, holding it across his palm. 'Don't do that, Miranda. You don't have to pretend. Not with me. We have no secrets. We know one another.' And then he bent and kissed her fingers, saluting her wounds as a badge of the courage she'd shown last night. 'We will always know one another.'

'I…'

He saw her throat move as she swallowed, for once lost for words.

He waited.

'I… Yes.' And it was not the sophisticated woman of the world but an echo of the shy young woman she must have been. 'Thank you.'

In danger of saying—doing—something that was totally out of place, he turned and looked up the shaft to the outside world. It seemed a very long way and, having seen the state of her hands, he wondered if she was up to this second climb.

If he was.

But he knew there was no point in suggesting she wait while he went for help.

'Are you ready?'

She nodded. Then said, 'No! Wait!'

And she took her tiny cellphone from her pocket, opened it and quickly entered a brief message. Then, when she saw him watching her, she started to shrug, stopped and said, 'It's not that I doubt we'll do this, Nick. But I could get knocked down crossing the road. Or the plane could—'

'Optimistic soul, aren't you?' he said.

'My parents were killed when the yacht they were on sank. They were just gone. Nothing.' She paused, looking up at him as if asking him to understand. 'Suddenly life seems very precious, Nick. I want the people I love to know how I'm feeling now. That I'm…happy.' And then she reached up, pressed her cheek to his. 'Thank you for last night. For listening. For knowing me…'

For a moment she was in his arms and they clung to one another. Any two people would do the same, he told himself. Except he knew it was more than that. They had connected in the darkness. Bonded. Exposed themselves in ways neither of them had ever done before.

What had happened had forced them to look at their lives, confront the dark spaces, consider a different future.

'Okay. I'm ready now,' she said, taking a step back.

He grabbed her wrist as she disturbed loose stones that, endless seconds later, clattered to the floor below, then, without a word, he took the phone from her and keyed in a message of his own before handing it back.

'I don't have a cell number for my father, so I've sent it via your brother…'

She smiled. 'You won't be sorry.'

He didn't answer, just said, 'I'll go first. Stick close. Whatever happens behind you, just keep going.'

Manda knew how to concentrate.

She concentrated her world into Nick's voice, giving her a running commentary of his moves. She concentrated on his feet, his boots, one step ahead of her. And, one move at a time, she finally found herself not so much climbing out of the shaft as falling, tumbling, rolling sideways down a steep slope until his body brought her to a halt.

He said nothing, just took her hand, and she lay still while she regained her breath. Only then did a giggle explode from her. They'd survived, overcome all the odds, made it back from the dead.

Somewhere above them in the canopy a bird, or maybe it was some small mammal, joined in, setting up a cacophony of raucous laughter that echoed around the forest.

It just made her laugh all the more.

'What?' Nick said, turning to look at her.

She just shook her head, unable to answer him, unable to do or say anything. Laughing so much that tears were pouring down her cheeks.

And after a moment his beautiful, strong, sensuous mouth—the one that looked as if it hadn't smiled in centuries—twitched in sympathetic response. Then widened into a smile and then he too was laughing.

Jago wasn't sure when Miranda's laughter tipped over into tears. It didn't surprise him. There were always two sides of any emotional roller-coaster and hers had been a dark ride. He just held her hand so that she knew he was there and, after a while, hiccupping, sniffling a little, she rubbed a sleeve over her cheek. Then looked at the once white linen, the smears where sweat and tears had mingled with dust, a little blood where a loose stone had caught her cheek.

'I'm filthy,' she said.

'You're gorgeous.'

She turned to look at him. 'So are you.'

'Filthy?'

'Filthy. Gorgeous. Gorgeously filthy. What we could both do with is a shower. You run a very slack establishment if you don't mind my saying so. I was lured to Cordillera with the promise of beautiful beaches, thrilling scenery and every comfort known to man.'

'Put your complaint in writing. I'll give you the name of the Minister of Tourism.' Then, because he didn't want to think about that, because he was alive and he didn't want to

feel bad about anyone—not Fliss, not even Felipe Dominez—
he said, 'In the meantime, if you can stagger a hundred yards
or so, I can offer you the basic facilities, always assuming that
nature hasn't messed with the plumbing.'

'Plumbing?'

'There's a stream at the bottom of this hill. Cold and cold
running water.'

'Water! What on earth are we waiting for?' She didn't
exactly leap up, but made a very good stab at it. She barely
winced as her knee buckled. 'Which way?'

He forced himself to his feet. 'This way,' he said, leading
her down through the mess of dead leaves and shattered
branches that littered the forest floor, towards the sound of
running water.

She was limping, he noticed and taking her hand to give
her support, he asked, 'How's your knee?'

'Thirsty.'

The walk down the steep path to the bottom of a small side
valley nearly finished them both, but the sight of water pouring
over a small waterfall and into a pool brought him to a halt.

'What is it?'

He shook his head. 'Nothing.' He'd expected change, devastation. 'Apart from a few leaves floating on the water, it
seems untouched…'

'Well, that's great,' she said, urging him on and as one, they
flung themselves down beside the pool, scooping up water in
their hands to slake their thirst.

Manda drank, splashed water over her face, then lay still,
her sore fingers trailing in the cool water.

'Better?' Nick asked.

'I didn't believe water could taste that good. Is it safe?' she
asked.

'I've been drinking it for five years without any ill effects. It comes from a spring just below the main building of the temple and I ran a standpipe to the site.'

'Maybe someone should bottle it.'

'Maybe they should.' He rolled on to his back. 'It was considered sacred by the people who lived here and the original temple building was built over it to protect it. Then, as the power of the tribe grew, new buildings were added and the water was channelled through them for cleansing rituals.'

'So why wasn't there any down in the basement, where we needed it?'

'Over centuries of neglect, the original spring gradually silted up. But water, being water, it found another way.' Then, 'Maybe we should make a move. There will be people looking for us.'

'We'll hear them,' she stalled, not wanting to move.

The pool was unbelievably beautiful. There were ferns growing where the water splashed on to the rocks. Tiny blue flowers, epiphytes growing in the misted air and huge ivory lilies that filled the air with their scent. Trees bearing berries that looked good enough to eat...

It felt untouched, new.

'You know those people, centuries ago, wasting all that time and energy building huge stone temples had it quite wrong.'

'They did?'

'You don't need stone to make a temple. This is the real deal. The sky, the earth. Fruit and flowers...' She stopped, her eye caught by a flash of shimmering colour as a dragonfly skimmed the pool. 'Water.'

She scooped up another mouthful and then, realising that it wasn't enough, she sat up and reached for her shirt buttons.

'Miranda? What are you doing?'

'I'm going to immerse myself. Soak in the water through

my skin. And then I'm going to indulge in a little cleansing ritual of my own.'

Her fingers were stiff and awkward and she doubted they'd be up to the task of refastening them, but she'd worry about that later. For now, her only goal was to totally rehydrate herself. Be clean.

Her bra proved more difficult and she turned her back to Jago.

'Are you going to just lie there and watch a woman struggle?' she demanded. Before he could make any kind of move, the hook gave way and she peeled it off, tossed it aside. She'd revealed the darkest secrets of her soul to this man, her body was nothing…

Jago could not take his eyes off her as she stripped off her clothes, transforming herself without a hint of self-consciousness into Eve, before she stepped carefully down into the clear water of the pool. Standing for a moment, as if soaking it up, before kicking off to swim across to the waterfall.

The water streamed from her shoulders as she stood up, turning her pale skin to ivory satin against the jet of her hair. And then she turned and looked over her shoulder at him and said, 'This is an equal opportunities cleansing ritual, Nick. There's plenty of room for two.'

CHAPTER ELEVEN

'COLD?'

Manda turned as Jago's broad shoulders emerged from the water to stand beside her beneath the waterfall.

He was lean, sinewy. There was nothing pampered or soft about him. No spare flesh. Lean, hard, with something gaunt, hollow-cheeked about the face that reminded her of an El Greco saint.

'Not now,' she said, and it was true. He did not have to smile to warm her, but when he did it was as if he'd switched on some internal central heating.

'Liar,' he said, ducking his head beneath the shower, dragging his fingers through his hair to shift the dust. And as he bent she saw the mass of purple bruising darkening his left shoulder, his shoulder blade, under his arm.

Without thinking, she reached out and touched him.

'Miranda,' he warned, straightening.

She took no notice but flattened her palms against the bruises as if trying to possess them, take them back. 'I'm sorry,' she said. 'I'm so sorry—'

'No!' He turned to face her, grabbing her, shaking her a little. 'You didn't do this, do you hear me? It just happened.

If I had dislocated it, broken it, if I had died attempting to save you it would not be your fault.'

'I know,' she said. And she did. 'I just wish I had something to make to better.'

They were close.

The water was cold, but Jago was not. 'There is something,' he said, lifting her from her feet and moving her closer so that there was nothing between them but a film of water that was rapidly heating up. 'Your warmth, Miranda Grenville. And, now that I can see it, your smile.'

She was smiling?

Actually, washed clean, with his body this close to hers, why wouldn't she be smiling?

'You want another kiss-it-better kiss, Nick Alexander Jago Jackson? Is that it?' She didn't wait for his answer. Her mouth was level with his shoulder, inches from his poor bruised skin, but, as she leaned into it, he backed off.

Startled, she looked up. 'Not this time,' he said. 'This is an equal opportunity healing ritual. I've been keeping count and it's my turn.' And, with his gaze fixed firmly on her mouth, he lowered his lips to hers.

She watched it happen in slow motion. Seeing everything. The sunlight filtering through the canopy sparkling on the drops of water clinging to his hair. A petal drifting from somewhere above them as the air stirred. Heard the beat of wings. And then she slammed her eyes shut. Saw nothing. Heard nothing. All her senses channelled into one.

Feeling.

His lips barely touched hers—no more than a promise—before moving on to the delicate skin behind her ears, her neck. His tongue traced the hollows of her collar-bone while his fingers eased across her shoulders, the nape of her neck and she discovered an unexpected erogenous zone. That bones truly could melt.

This was not a kissing-it-better kiss. Manda might not know much, but she knew that. This was a make-the-world-go-away kiss that drew from her soft purring sighs that didn't sound like any sound she'd ever made in her entire life.

He kissed every part of her, bringing life flooding to her breasts, blowing softly into her navel as he laid her back in the water to expose more of her body to his lips. Keeping her safe with one powerful arm as he took the concept of kissing-it-better and lifted it to an entirely different plane.

Then, with her shoulders nestled into the soft moss of the bank, she drew him to her, telling him with every touch, every murmur that she wanted more and he gave her himself so completely, so selflessly, waiting and waiting for her, that afterwards she lay in his arms, tears of gratitude in her eyes. Reborn. Renewed.

'Are you hungry?' he asked as they lay on the grass, recovering.

'Starving. Shall we be greedy and eat all the mints?'

'I can do better than that.' He got up and swam across the pool to the waterfall and then began to climb up the rocks to pick the berries that grew there.

'Be careful,' she called out, more nervous now than in the bowels of the temple. But she hadn't been able to see the danger there. Hadn't been able to see him. Or that hideous bruise.

He just smiled and turned, but she couldn't bear to watch and she decided to get dressed.

She recoiled from her underwear and instead slipped into her trousers, then pulled her shirt over her naked skin. Unfortunately, her fingers and the buttons didn't want to co-operate and she was still struggling with them when Nick returned.

'Give me your hands.'

'I just need to—'

'I'll see to it when we've eaten. Here, take them.' He tipped a handful of berries into her hands. 'I've no idea what these are, but they're very high in sugar. The locals dry them and use them for long journeys.'

She tried one. He was right, they were sweet. 'They're very good,' she said, holding them for him to help himself. 'But then I'm so hungry that deadly nightshade would probably taste good right now.'

'Try a little brandy with them.'

'This is a picnic? We can finish it off with the last of the mints.'

After they'd eaten and washed their hands in the pool, they lay side by side, just letting the sun warm them, saying nothing. What was there left to say? They both knew that what had happened had been the final act in a drama that had overtaken them.

Except, of course, for the elephant in the room.

It was Nick who finally broke the silence.

'Miranda—'

She rolled over, putting her fingers on his mouth before he could say the words. 'You're safe, Nick. That's the first time for me in ten years.'

'Ten years? A life sentence,' he said, holding her, kissing her damp hair, her forehead, her cheek, until she had no choice but to look up at him. 'I can't match that kind of celibacy, but I've always used protection. Until today.'

'Today was different. This is the Garden of Eden before the Fall.'

'Maybe, but even the most basic biology lesson would confirm that unprotected sex, wherever it happens, can lead to pregnancy.'

'No.' It was her last secret. Telling him would be like removing the final veil. Leaving her stripped bare, exposed in a way that simple nakedness had not. 'Not for me. The ectopic pregnancy made a bit of a mess when it ruptured, Nick. I will never have a child of my own.'

'I'm sorry.'

That was the thing about learning to control your own feelings—you recognised the real thing when you saw it. When Jago said those two little words, he meant it. Not in a pitying way. But because he understood how much she had lost. Understood everything.

He'd saved her life, brought her from the darkness, given her back the simple joy of her body and with those two words she knew that it would be the easiest thing in the world to fall in love with him.

It was time, in other words, to slip the mask back into place. Not to hide hurt. If she never saw him again after today it would be a cause for regret, but not for pain. He had given her more than he could ever know.

He had been compassionate, kind and, in giving her his own very special version of the kiss of life, he had, quite unknowingly, lifted that dark shadow from her life. The fear that her love was not good enough.

She had trusted him and he had not let her down and now she could trust herself. Trust the love she had been yearning to give and, instead of locking it away, scared of rejection, she would use it. First she'd reassure herself that the child they'd found—Rosie—was safe and happy. Do something for the other children out there, the ones whose thin and grubby little faces hadn't made it into print.

She would wear her mask lightly, and only to protect him from any vestige of guilt for not loving her.

She'd been aware for some time of the sound of a helicopter quartering the ground nearby and she said, 'Time to move, I think. If you'd deal with the buttons?'

'We could just stay here,' Jago replied, keeping a firm hold of her hand. 'Live on nuts and wild berries.'

'We could,' she agreed. 'But I have a documentary to produce and you have a book to write. The real story about the people who lived here.'

'It won't be a sex and sandals bestseller.'

'It will be the truth. You owe them that and I promise I'll be at the head of the line when you have your first book signing.'

'That's an incentive,' he said and his smile formed deep lines down his cheeks. 'Although academic authors tend not to make it out of their own university bookshop.'

'Maybe the rubbish book will provoke interest.'

'Maybe it will. I might sell three more copies.'

'Just tell me where and I'll bring everyone I know. We'll have a party.'

'If I do, will you invite me to the first screening of your documentary?'

She hesitated. 'It's about broken families, Nick. Adoption. The search for birth families. Reunion.'

'Stories which don't always have a happy-ever-after ending?' he suggested. 'Is that why you won't follow up the little girl in your last documentary? In case her story doesn't have a happy ending.'

'I…' She swallowed. 'Yes.' Then, meeting grey eyes that refused to accept anything less than total honesty, 'I've let her down, haven't I?'

'You wanted to believe she was happy. When you're afraid that reality might not live up to your dream, it's tempting to stay where it's safe.'

'With the dream.' She looked around at the perfect vision of paradise that surrounded them. It was lovely for a few hours stolen from life, but the scent that had at first seemed so sweet was now making her drowsy. Was that what the scent of the lilies did? Drug the senses... 'Maybe I've always been hung up on the dream, instead of accepting reality. Yearning for the fairy tale and missing what was in front of me.'

She turned to confront this man who'd given her back her life, both literally and emotionally.

'Isn't that what you've been doing too, Nick? Sticking with the dream of your perfect family, perfect parents. Unable to see your mother and father as just two ordinary people with ordinary frailties. Just like everyone else.'

She didn't wait for him to answer. The question was rhetorical, something for him to think about. Instead, she removed her hand from his and, making a move for her shirt buttons, said, 'It's time to leave, Nick.'

As she fumbled awkwardly, he reached out and stopped her. 'I said I'd do that.'

For a moment Jago thought Miranda was going to resist this final intimacy.

But then she smiled and let her hands drop to her lap. It was a simple gesture of trust and he fastened them carefully, without touching her, knowing that this simple act represented closure. An end to what had happened between them. On an impulse he said, 'I've got an idea.'

She glanced up as a shadow passed over them, a blast of noise, a shower of leaves. The helicopter, directly overhead now. Beneath the canopy they were invisible from the air, but even so it would not be long before the world crashed in on them and, as soon as the beating of the rotor faded, he said, 'Let's come back here. A year from today. No matter what. You bring a packet of mints. I'll bring a bottle of local brandy and we can pick berries. Have a feast. Maybe stay all night, gather lilies to put on a bonfire, give thanks for our deliverance.'

She smiled and for a moment he thought she was going to say that they should stay here now, for ever. But then she seemed to gather herself and, staggering to her feet, shook her head and said, 'The lilies… Did you ever consider they might have some kind of narcotic effect?'

In other words, no.

'Look, can we get out of here?'

She didn't wait, but bundled her underwear, the bottle and sweet wrappers into her ruined bag and slung it over her shoulder and walked quickly up the slope to where, even now, he could hear people shouting her name. His name. Maybe he'd been a little hard on Felipe Dominez.

Leaving him and the glade as apparently untouched as before she'd burst into his life.

He dressed and followed her, reassured the searchers that there was no one left in the shattered building in which they'd spent the night. By the time he reached the clearing where he'd left his Land Rover—now lying on its side at the bottom of a gully, along with the remains of the tour bus—she had been swallowed up by her fellow tourists.

They surrounded her, exclaiming over her, hugging her, treasuring her as someone who'd returned from the dead. Then, before he could join her, he heard his own name ring out.

'Jago!'

And then he had his arms full of woman as Fliss flung herself at him.

'You're alive!'

'Apparently,' he said, putting her down, holding her off. 'I didn't expect to see you here again.'

She had the grace to look embarrassed. 'Felipe wanted photographs of me at the temple. And I wanted to explain about the book. You have heard about the book?'

'Yes, I heard. I hope it's listed under fiction.'

'Jago...' She looked at him, all big eyes and hot lips. There was no doubt about it, she was one hell of a female and despite what she'd done, he grinned.

'What are you doing here, Fliss? Really?'

'When the earthquake hit, everyone was running around like headless chickens. If you were outside the capital...' She shrugged. 'I told Felipe that if he didn't do something I'd tell everyone the truth. That the book was cooked up by some ghost-writer—'

'And then he realised that this place was full of tourists who had families and he actually gave a damn.'

'Well, maybe. I'm sorry, Jago. About the book. Truly.'

'Truly, Fliss, you're not cut out to be an archaeologist and you saw an easy way to make some money. Get the celebrity lifestyle. It's okay. I don't care about the book.'

All he cared about was Miranda, already being ushered towards the waiting helicopter with the other women, some of the older men. He needed to get to her, to say something, tell her...

'You forgive me?' Fliss persisted.

'Yes, yes...' he said impatiently as, over her head, he saw Miranda look back and for a moment hold his gaze.

Manda had practically fled from the glade, afraid of what she might say. Knowing that a year from now they would be different people. That to try and recapture this precious, almost perfect moment would be a mistake.

She wasn't running away from her feelings or protecting herself—she would never do that again. Just running towards real life. Hoping, maybe, that in his own good time he'd follow her. Might remember his promise to invite her to his first book signing.

But then, as she'd stumbled into the clearing, she'd been surrounded by the rest of the tour group, who'd apparently been sheltering in one of the buildings, waiting for rescue. Believing that she was dead.

Being bustled towards the waiting helicopter along with her fellow tourists. Knowing that to delay would be to hold them up when they were desperate for food, hot water and sleep.

Except she could step back, let one of the men take her place and, as the rest of the party pushed by her, eager to get aboard, she glanced back, seeking him out.

For a moment she couldn't see Jago and took a step back. But then she caught a glimpse of his tousled black mop of hair as he lifted his head so that he was standing a little taller than everyone else, right on the edge of the group, and she realised that he'd been talking to someone.

The bus driver, perhaps. He probably knew everyone…

'Miss, can you get in, please…'

On the point of surrendering her seat to someone else— there was a general movement as those remaining were ushered clear of the rotor blades—she saw the someone Nick was talking to. Not the driver, not a man, but the curvy blonde who she'd last seen poured into a clinging gown and flirting with a chat show host on the television. As she stood there Nick said something and then, as if feeling her eyes on him, he glanced up and for a moment held her gaze. Still held it as the woman— Fliss, she had a name—flung herself into his arms.

And, for one last time, she dug deep for the smile that had hidden her feelings for so long. Smiled, mouthed, 'thank you' before turning quickly and climbing aboard the helicopter.

She was the last one to board and the door was immediately slammed behind her. It took off almost immediately.

Manda kept her eyes closed as it hovered above the clearing, resisting the temptation to look down, look back. Then, as it cleared the trees, banked and headed into the sun, she opened them and made a promise to herself.

This was a new beginning and from now on it was only forwards, only positive. There would still be dark moments, but she would never again wrap them around her like a cape, but work through them to the light, knowing it would, like the dawn, like spring, always return.

Then they neared the coast and her phone beeped to let her know that she had incoming messages. She flipped it open and read the urgent, desperate messages from Ivo, Belle, Daisy who had, no doubt, been contacted by the consul when the hotel had posted her amongst the missing.

And she hit send on the stored messages that she'd written in the dark, when survival had not been certain. Simple messages that told them how much she loved them.

And then, because it was too noisy to talk, she keyed in another to tell her brother that she was safe. That she was on her way home.

Jago disentangled himself from the embrace of Fliss Grant and watched the helicopter turn and head for the coast, taking Miranda away from him.

'How did you get up here?' he asked.

'I drove up in that Jeep.' She pointed out a Jeep with the Government insignia and a driver. 'The road's a bit torn up but it's passable.'

'And the village?'

'Not much damage. A few minor injuries, that's all.'

'Good. I need to pick up my things and get to the coast.'

'You're leaving? You won't get a flight. It's chaos at the airport.'

That meant that Miranda couldn't leave either. 'Just drop me at the new resort.'

'No problem. I'm staying there myself.'

'Fliss, the book I can forgive, but, as for the rest, I'd advise you to stick to Felipe. He's your kind of man.' With that, he swung himself into the Jeep and said, 'Let's get out of here.'

Manda showered, changed and, less than an hour after leaving the temple site, she was boarding a helicopter that Ivo had chartered to pick her up from the resort and fly her to a nearby island where he had a private jet waiting.

He might have stepped back a little from the twenty-four/seven world he'd once occupied, but her brother still knew how to make things happen.

The village might not have been badly hit, but the people still needed help. This had been his home for the best part of five years and Jago couldn't just walk away.

It was a week before he finally made it on to a jet that would take him home. And the first person he saw when he walked through to arrivals was his father.

Older, a little thinner, a lot greyer. For a moment they just stood and looked at one another.

Then his father said, 'Ivo Grenville called me. Passed on your message. Your mother…' He stopped, unable to speak.

'Where is she?' he asked. Then, fear seizing him by the throat, 'Is she ill?'

'No, son. She stayed in the car. She knew she'd cry and she remembers how much you hate that.'

If he'd had any doubts about his promise to Miranda, they were shattered in that moment when he thought he might have left it too late.

'My first day at school. I was telling someone about that only the other day. Miranda. Ivo Grenville's sister.'

'You were trapped with her, Ivo said. I met her once. She's was a tremendous help with one of my projects.'

'She didn't say.' He thought he understood why. 'Will you call Ivo, ask him to thank her for me? For sending the message.'

His father regarded him thoughtfully. 'I think maybe you should do that yourself.'

'I will. Soon. But if you call, she'll know I've kept my word.'

He nodded. Then, 'Shall we go and brave the waterworks?'

'I think perhaps I've finally grown up enough to handle a few tears,' he said. And he flung an arm around his father and hugged him.

It had taken the best part of two months to finish the filming of the new documentary and it was finally in the can. Finished.

Manda sat at her desk tapping the phone with her pen. She'd promised to invite Nick to the private screening. Was it a good idea?

What they'd shared had been no more than a moment in time. A life-changing moment, a moment to cherish, but to try and carry it into everyday life…

She knew he'd seen his parents. His father had called Ivo, asked him to pass on his thanks to her, but he hadn't called her himself even though he was back in London, no doubt working on his book. But then she hadn't called him.

Of course she'd been busy. She'd driven all over the country with Belle and Daisy, putting the adoption documentary together.

No doubt Nick was busy, too. And presumably Fliss Grant was keeping him fully occupied out of working hours. She'd certainly dropped out of the celebrity gossip mag circuit.

Actually, despite the enthusiastic welcome Fliss had received from Nick when she'd turned up with the rescue team, Manda was a little surprised by that.

For a man who held truth in such high regard, it seemed out of character for him to forgive that kind of betrayal.

She dragged her mind back from the memory of the magical moments they'd spent at the forest pool. Maybe that was the lesson Nick had learned in those long hours they'd spent together in the dark. That life is too short. That you had to grab it with both hands, take what it offered. Move on. Looking forward, never back.

Something she was doing herself. Mostly. Not forgetting, she would never forget Nick Jago. He had given her back her life, was part of every waking moment. He always would be; it was something that made her smile rather than cry.

'I'm leaving now, Manda,' Daisy said, wheeling in the stroller containing her sleeping baby. 'We'll be at Wardour Street at eight.'

It took her a moment to readjust to the present. 'Eight? Oh, right. What's the final headcount?'

'I think we've just about got a full house.'

'Well, that's great. Thank you. You've done a great job.' And, glad of an excuse to put off making a decision about whether to call Nick, she dropped the pen on her desk and bent to croon over her sleeping godson.

'Hi, Jude. You just get more gorgeous every day.'

'Manda…'

She looked up, saw trouble. 'What's up?'

'This is a bad time to tell you, but there's never going to be a good one.'

'What?' Then, because she knew the answer, 'It's Rosie, isn't it?'

'You asked me to find out what happened to her.'

'And?'

'It's not good, I'm afraid. You know that she was being held in a care home for assessment while they found a family who would be able to cope? Most of the couples who wanted her didn't have the first clue about what they'd be taking on.'

None of that was relevant and she dismissed it with an impatient gesture. 'She's gone, hasn't she? How long?'

'Months.'

'And they didn't bother to tell us?'

'Manda…'

'I know, I know,' she said, waving away the jargon. She'd heard it all since she'd joined up with Belle to help raise the profile of her causes. 'It's none of our business. No doubt there are laws. Privacy. All that stuff…'

'Yes, there are, but I think the real problem was that they were afraid you'd go to the press. Make them look bad. You can be a bit…well…intimidating.'

'Really?' She combed her hair back with her fingers. 'I don't mean to be. I just don't—'

'—suffer fools gladly. I know. If it helps, you never scared me.'

That was a fact. But then Daisy had been little more than a street brat herself. Full of lip. Terrified beneath all that front. They were total opposites and yet there had been a kind of recognition…

'I have to find her, Daisy. I need to find her.'

'I'll put out the word. It'll take time. If she doesn't want to be found…' She left Manda to fill in the rest. 'I'll catch up with you this evening at the screening.'

'Right.' Then, casually as she could, 'Actually, before you go, would you see if you can find a number for Dr Nicholas Jago, at the University of London?'

'The guy you were holed up with in that temple?'

'Yes.' She avoided Daisy's gaze, picking up her pen again, making a pretence of jotting down a note. 'We talked about the documentary and he said he'd like to see it. He was probably just being polite, but it won't hurt to give him a call and invite him along to the screening tonight.'

'Okay.'

'Tell him that he's welcome to bring a guest.'

The screening was for the network chiefs, the press, overseas buyers. After the awards they'd picked up for their first documentary, there had been considerable interest in the new film and Manda had laid on a buffet and a well stocked bar to keep the hacks happy.

She left Belle and Ivo to greet their guests—she was their 'face' after all—and kept herself busy with the money men. She'd positioned herself with her back to the door, determined not to be caught watching for Nick.

According to Daisy, he'd said he'd be delighted to come. But 'delighted' might just be being polite. Or maybe Daisy was being kind.

Neither Belle nor Daisy had said a word about the fact that she'd been trapped in the dark with a good-looking man for fifteen hours. Which suggested they suspected that the two of them had connected in some way.

Fortunately, she was still scary enough that neither of them had dared broach the subject.

Daisy hadn't said whether he was bringing a guest and Manda didn't ask.

'Manda?'

She turned as Daisy touched her arm, excusing herself, gladly, from a monologue on the necessity of tax incentives for film-makers.

'What's up?'

'Nothing. I could see you were glazing over, but I've been thinking about Rosie. She'd go back to the places she knew. Where she felt safe. I just thought…'

'What?' But Daisy's attention had been caught by something behind her and she turned to see what it was.

A man. Tall, dark, freshly barbered and shaved.

'Nick…' His name caught in her throat.

'Hello, Miranda.'

Daisy waited for an introduction but she couldn't speak and, after a moment, she said, 'I'll…um…go and start shepherding people through, shall I?' Then, to herself, 'Yes, Daisy, you do that…'

'You look… different,' Manda finally managed. 'In a suit.'

'Good different, or bad different?'

'Good.' In a dark bespoke suit, shirt unbuttoned at the neck, the kind of tan that was so deep it would never completely fade, he made everyone else present look stitched up, dull. No wonder Daisy had been staring… 'Not that you looked bad…' Oh, good grief. So much for walking away, not looking back, just being grateful for that one day. Sophisticated, scary Manda Grenville was behaving like a fifteen-year-old who'd just been smiled at by the hottest guy in school. '…before.'

'Without a suit.'

Without any clothes at all.

She peeled her tongue from the roof of her mouth, rounded up a few brain cells and finally managed a slightly hoarse, 'How's your shoulder?' It wasn't sparkling conversation, but it was safer than the pictures in her head of Nick Jago naked beneath a waterfall. Nick Jago with his mouth…

'How are you, Miranda?'

'Fine,' she said. 'Absolutely great. Working hard, but… great.'

'No nightmares?'

'No…' No nightmares. Just hot, hot dreams… 'You?'

'No nightmares,' he confirmed. 'Just dreams. Did you get my message?'

'Ivo told me. Yes. How is it? With your family?'

'They've changed. I've met my half-sister, too. I've you to thank for that.'

'You'd have got there.' Then the hard question. 'Are you on your own? Didn't Daisy tell you that you could bring someone.'

'Why would I bring someone, Miranda,' he said, 'when the only person I'm interested in being with is here already?'

'Really?' Trying to be cool when you needed a cold shower was never easy, but she did her best, looking around the widest shoulders in the room before saying, 'I haven't spotted the slinky blonde.'

And finally he smiled. As if she'd just told him everything he wanted to know. Well, she had…

'Fliss made her bed with Felipe Dominez, Miranda. I advised her to lie on it. I'd have told you that if you'd hung around for another thirty seconds.'

'Oh.'

'And you could have thanked her. It was down to her that the rescue services reached us so quickly.'

So Fliss Grant was in love with him, Manda thought,

feeling almost sorry for the woman. If he'd loved her in return she would never have written the book…

'Did she give you back your documents?'

It wouldn't hurt to remind him of what she'd done.

'There was no need. I had backup copies of everything. She knew that.'

'Of course you did.' Then, 'So, here you are. Finally. It took you two months to make up my head start of thirty seconds?'

'I got held up in the village. It was my home for nearly five years…'

'I'm sorry, Nick. Of course you had to stay. Was it terrible?'

'No. Just a bit of a mess. Nothing that hard work and a few dollars couldn't fix.'

'Money that you supplied.'

He shrugged. 'It was nothing. I stayed for a week, made sure everything was back on track for them, that's all.'

Far from all, she suspected…

'And then?'

'And then…' He looked at her for a moment, the smallest smile creasing the corners of his mouth, his eyes. 'And then, my dearest heart, we both had things to do. Everything happened so fast between us.'

'Was it fast? It seemed like a lifetime, everything slowed down…'

'Facing death, everything becomes concentrated, intense. We needed time to catch up. Time with our families. Time for work.' He took her hand, slid his fingers through hers. 'The future was waiting for us. We've finally caught up with it.' Then, 'Are you free after the screening? Can we have dinner? Talk?'

'Talk? What about?'

'Book signings. Your documentary. The fact that you knew my father and never told me. The rest of our lives.'

The rest of their lives?

She opened her mouth, closed it again.

'The rest of our lives?' she repeated. Then shook her head. 'No… You can't…'

'I've spent the last two months thinking about you in every waking hour. Dreaming about you in every sleeping one. And the truth is, Miranda, I can't not. I want to be with you. Always. Marry me.'

'Manda? We're about to begin.'

She looked round, realised that the room was empty apart from Daisy, who was holding the screening room door open.

'Go ahead without me,' she said.

'But…'

'I'll catch the rerun, Daisy. Right now, I've got the rest of my life to plan.'

They found a small Italian bistro nearby. Manda couldn't have said what she ate, or how it tasted, or even what they talked about. Only that they talked and laughed and that suddenly everything was in its place.

When they finally emerged into the chill of the December night, Christmas lights everywhere, Nick said, 'How did you get here?'

'By cab.'

'Me too.' He looked up and down the street. 'We're not likely to pick one up here at this time of night.' He held out his elbow and she tucked her arm around his. 'Which way?'

'It doesn't matter,' she said, in no hurry to find a cab, let go of this moment. End the evening. 'What will you do now?' she asked as they began to walk.

'I've been offered a chair at the university.'

'Here in London?' She thought about Cordillera. The wildness of the rainforest. A magical pool where a man and woman could pretend they were in Eden. 'It would be very different from what you're used to. Won't you miss fieldwork?'

'The aching back, the lack of basic facilities, the shortage of funding?'

'The magic moment when you find something that's a piece of the jigsaw,' she prompted, not believing him for a moment. 'That helps bring the picture of ancient lives into focus?'

He glanced at her. 'I'd still get my hands dirty once in a while,' he said. 'Not in Cordillera. The structures are not safe. But we're running other sites. And the slightly higher than average profile I've achieved, thanks to the earthquake, will be a big help in raising funds.'

'So? You're going to take it?'

He shrugged. 'I'm waiting for the right incentive package.'

'Oh.' They turned into a major shopping street. A cab stopped outside a restaurant to disgorge its passengers. They ignored it. Walked on. 'What kind of incentive would it take?'

'I'll know when I hear it.' He glanced at her. 'What about you? Where do you go from here?'

She shook her head, coming back to the real world. 'I can't think of anything but Rosie at the moment.'

'The little girl you rescued?'

Manda stopped.

'What's the matter?'

'She ran away, Nick. Months ago. I only found out today.' Her breath condensed in the freezing air. 'She's out here somewhere, in the city.' Then, looking around, realised where she was. 'Oh, God. This is where we found her. Just down here.'

And she pulled away and ran down a side alley, coming to an abrupt halt as she saw the Dumpster. For one crazy moment she'd thought she be there, digging around for food.

She turned and laid her face against Nick's coat as he caught up with her, put his arms around her.

'She'll die, Nick. I've let her down. I should have been there.'

'Shh.' She felt his breath against her hair as he kissed her, but she pulled away.

'Rosie! Do you hear me?' she called. 'I'm not giving up on you. I'll come back tomorrow. Search every alleyway in London if I have to, but you will not die, do you hear me?'

She clapped her hands over her mouth. Shook her head. Tears freezing on her cheeks.

'Manda…'

'What?' she asked crossly, rubbing a glove across her face. Then she realised that he wasn't looking at her but over her head and swung round, caught her breath as she saw the small, defiant figure standing glaring at them.

'Rosie?'

'Is he your boyfriend?' she demanded.

Manda swallowed.

He'd said 'the rest of our lives' but it was too soon for anything except knowing how much she had missed him. How much she wanted him to stay. How much she loved him.

'This is Nick, Rosie,' she said, grabbing all of those things and putting them together. 'He saved my life.'

'What did he do?'

'I was falling, down into a horrible dark place, but he held on to me even when he might have fallen too. And I'm here to hold on to you.' She crossed to the Dumpster, put her hand on the lid. 'Hungry?' she asked, knowing that she was going to have to open it. Knowing that she would do anything. Then, remembering something that Belle had told her about living on the streets as a child—the one thing they'd have given anything for—she said, 'Or maybe you'd like to come to my place and I'll make you a bacon sandwich. With ketchup.'

'Is your boyfriend coming?'

Nick Jago looked at this beautiful woman. He'd loved her before he'd even seen her, he realised, his heart stolen by the mixture of strength, vulnerability—something more that made her everything she was. Then, when he'd seen her, his eyes had confirmed everything his heart had already known. It was as if his entire world had been shaken to bits and then, when it had been put back together, everything had somehow fallen into place. And then she had gone, whirled away from him in a helicopter before he could say the words. Still running?

He didn't know, but he'd given her space, given himself space for the whirlwind of feelings to be blown away.

But it hadn't happened. Sometimes, in the darkest moment, you met your destiny and he knew, without doubt, that she was his.

'I'm not Miranda's boyfriend, Rosie,' he said, moving to join her. 'I'm the man she's going to marry.'

And when Miranda turned to stare at him, he held her gaze, daring her to deny it. She didn't. Her silence was all he needed and, taking off his coat, he said, 'You know that incentive to stay in London that I was talking about?'

She just nodded as he wrapped it around the freezing child.

'I just heard it.'

'Rosie!' Her room was empty. Her bed not slept in. Manda didn't know what had woken her, only that she'd known, instantly, that Rosie had run again. She turned as Nick joined her in the bedroom doorway. 'She's gone, Nick.'

It had been six months. It hadn't been easy, but they'd

made it and, now that Social Services were ready to approve their adoption, she'd been certain they were through the worst. And Rosie had been so excited about being their bridesmaid.

Now, with the wedding less than a week away, she'd run again.

She turned to Nick and buried her face in his chest. 'What now?'

'I think she may have started taking food again,' Nick said. 'I thought maybe she was just a little unsettled—about staying with Daisy while we're on our honeymoon.'

It had taken a while before she'd trusted them enough to stop taking stuff from the fridge to keep in her bag.

'But she adores Daisy. Can't wait to stay with her and Jude next week. I thought she was sure of us. Settled.'

There had been problems before, when they'd set the date for the wedding. She'd run away then too, afraid that they'd have babies of their own and wouldn't want her any more.

But when Nick had told her that wasn't going to happen, had explained that Manda couldn't have children of her own, she'd seemed to settle.

'Don't panic, Miranda. She always goes back to the same place. We'll go and pick her up and get to the bottom of this.' Then, frowning, 'Did you hear something?'

'It sounded like the back door. Burglars?'

Rosie's fiercely whispered 'Shh…' answered that question.

'The kitchen?' Nick suggested.

They opened the door. Rosie had her head in the fridge and didn't see them. The small boy, sitting on one of the kitchen stools, almost smothered by one of Rosie's padded jackets, leapt to his feet, knocking over a mug tree, sending crockery flying as he bolted for the door.

Nick cut him off, scooped him up, holding him easily,

despite his desperate struggle. He was about five years old, his mop of black hair a matted tangle and skinny as a lath, but he had huge dark eyes and the kind of beauty that would melt hearts at twenty paces.

Nick smiled at him, tucked him up against his chest and said, 'Who's your friend, Rosie?'

She closed the fridge door very slowly, then turned to face them. 'He was eating out of the bins behind the supermarket. I saw him the other day and I took him some stuff. Clothes, food. On my way to school.'

'You should have told us,' Manda said.

'I thought maybe his mum would come back for him. Sometimes they just get out of their heads for a while, but then they come back. Like my mum did.'

Until, eventually, she didn't, Manda thought.

'But she didn't.' Rosie's shrug was a mixture of defiance and pleading. 'I waited a week and then I thought, since you can't have kids of your own, he should come and live with us. I'll need a brother,' she added a little defiantly.

'Does he have a name?' Nick asked.

'He's called Michael.'

'Rosie,' Manda cut in as gently as she could, 'you know it's not that easy. I'll have to call Social Services. He may have a family…'

'The kind that leaves him on the street. I had family like that too.'

'Even so.'

'I know.' She sighed. 'There are rules and stuff. But you can fix it. You and Nick can fix anything and, besides, you said it was a pity Jude wasn't old enough to be a page-boy.'

'So I did,' Manda said, turning helplessly to the gorgeous man who'd swept her up in a whirlwind of love, made her a family of her own. 'Nick? Do you have any thoughts about how we can handle this?'

He grinned and said, 'I always think best with a bacon sandwich in front of me.' He looked at the child in his arms. 'Michael?'

And Manda felt Rosie's hand creep into hers.

Five days later, Miranda Grenville and Nicholas Jago were married in a centuries-old London church that had been designed by Christopher Wren.

It was one of those rare perfect June days when, even in London, the flower-filled parks still wore the freshness of early summer.

As Miranda emerged from a vintage Rolls Royce on her brother's arm, she paused for a moment while Belle and Daisy, her attendants, straightened the train of the simplest, most elegant ivory silk gown, giving the paparazzi time to take their photographs. This was, after all, the society wedding of the year.

Nothing could have been further from the circumstances of their meeting in Cordillera. Everything pristine, perfect.

Rosie, gorgeous in primrose and white organza, was almost beside herself with excitement. Michael, his hand clutched firmly in hers, was bemused in a tiny kilt and ruffles.

The plan had been to go back, visit their pool, light their fire but they'd put their honeymoon on hold until they'd settled Michael's future.

'Ready?' Ivo asked.

She took a deep breath and said, 'Not quite. I just wanted to say…' She had a load of words, but in the end it came down to two. 'Thank you.' She didn't have to say what for. They both knew. 'Now I'm ready.'

Rosie and Michael led the way, scattering rose petals before them as, to the strains of Pachelbel's *Canon*, Manda walked down the flower-decked aisle towards the man she loved.

She saw nothing, was aware of nothing but Nick waiting for her, his smile telling her that he thought he was the most fortunate man in the world.

Him, and the warm, spicy scent of the huge trumpet lilies entwined along the altar rail. Cordilleran lilies.

'You had them flown in especially?' she murmured as he took her hand.

'We couldn't go to Cordillera, so I brought it to us and tonight I'll light a fire that will keep us both warm for as long as we both shall live.'

* * * * *

Here is a sneak preview of
A STONE CREEK CHRISTMAS,
the latest in Linda Lael Miller's acclaimed
McKETTRICK *series.*

A lonely horse brought vet Olivia O'Ballivan to Tanner
Quinn's farm, but it's the rancher's love that might cause
her to stay.

A STONE CREEK CHRISTMAS
Available December 2008
from Silhouette Special Edition

Tanner heard the rig roll in around sunset. Smiling, he wandered to the window. Watched as Olivia O'Ballivan climbed out of her Suburban, flung one defiant glance toward the house and started for the barn, the golden retriever trotting along behind her.

Taking his coat and hat down from the peg next to the back door, he put them on and went outside. He was used to being alone, even liked it, but keeping company with Doc O'Ballivan, bristly though she sometimes was, would provide a welcome diversion.

He gave her time to reach the horse Butterpie's stall, then walked into the barn.

The golden retriever came to greet him, all wagging tail and melting brown eyes, and he bent to stroke her soft, sturdy back. "Hey, there, dog," he said.

Sure enough, Olivia was in the stall, brushing Butterpie down and talking to her in a soft, soothing voice that touched something private inside Tanner and made him want to turn on one heel and beat it back to the house.

He'd be damned if he'd do it, though.

This was *his* ranch, *his* barn. Well-intentioned as she was, *Olivia* was the trespasser here, not him.

"She's still very upset," Olivia told him, without turning to look at him or slowing down with the brush.

Shiloh, always an easy horse to get along with, stood contentedly in his own stall, munching away on the feed Tanner had given him earlier. Butterpie, he noted, hadn't touched her supper as far as he could tell.

"Do you know anything at all about horses, Mr. Quinn?" Olivia asked.

He leaned against the stall door, the way he had the day before, and grinned. He'd practically been raised on horseback; he and Tessa had grown up on their grandmother's farm in the Texas hill country, after their folks divorced and went their separate ways, both of them too busy to bother with a couple of kids. "A few things," he said. "And I mean to call you Olivia, so you might as well return the favor and address me by my first name."

He watched as she took that in, dealt with it, decided on an approach. He'd have to wait and see what that turned out to be, but he didn't mind. It was a pleasure just watching Olivia O'Ballivan grooming a horse.

"All right, *Tanner,*" she said. "This barn is a disgrace. When are you going to have the roof fixed? If it snows again, the hay will get wet and probably mold…"

He chuckled, shifted a little. He'd have a crew out there the following Monday morning to replace the roof and shore up the walls—he'd made the arrangements over a week before—but he felt no particular compunction to explain that. He was enjoying her ire too much; it made her color rise and her hair fly when she turned her head, and the faster breathing made her perfect breasts go up and down in an enticing rhythm. "What makes you so sure I'm a greenhorn?" he asked mildly, still leaning on the gate.

At last she looked straight at him, but she didn't move from Butterpie's side. "Your hat, your boots—that fancy red truck you drive. I'll bet it's customized."

Tanner grinned. Adjusted his hat. "Are you telling me real cowboys don't drive red trucks?"

"There are lots of trucks around here," she said. "Some of them are red, and some of them are new. And *all* of them are splattered with mud or manure or both."

"Maybe I ought to put in a car wash, then," he teased. "Sounds like there's a market for one. Might be a good investment."

She softened, though not significantly, and spared him a cautious half smile, full of questions she probably wouldn't ask. "There's a good car wash in Indian Rock," she informed him. "People go there. It's only forty miles."

"Oh," he said with just a hint of mockery. "*Only* forty miles. Well, then. Guess I'd better dirty up my truck if I want to be taken seriously in these here parts. Scuff up my boots a bit, too, and maybe stomp on my hat a couple of times."

Her cheeks went a fetching shade of pink. "You are twisting what I said," she told him, brushing Butterpie again, her touch gentle but sure. "I meant…"

Tanner envied that little horse. Wished he had a furry hide, so he'd need brushing, too.

"You *meant* that I'm not a real cowboy," he said. "And you could be right. I've spent a lot of time on construction sites over the last few years, or in meetings where a hat and boots wouldn't be appropriate. Instead of digging out my old gear, once I decided to take this job, I just bought new."

"I bet you don't even *have* any old gear," she challenged, but she was smiling, albeit cautiously, as though she might withdraw into a disapproving frown at any second.

He took off his hat, extended it to her. "Here," he teased. "Rub that around in the muck until it suits you."

She laughed, and the sound—well, it caused a powerful and wholly unexpected shift inside him. Scared the hell out of him and, paradoxically, made him yearn to hear it again.

* * * * *

*Discover how this rugged rancher's wanderlust is tamed
in time for a merry Christmas, in
A STONE CREEK CHRISTMAS.
In stores December 2008.*

SPECIAL EDITION™

**FROM *NEW YORK TIMES*
BESTSELLING AUTHOR**

LINDA LAEL MILLER

A STONE CREEK CHRISTMAS

Veterinarian Olivia O'Ballivan finds the animals
in Stone Creek playing Cupid between her and
Tanner Quinn. Even Tanner's daughter, Sophie,
is eager to play matchmaker. With everyone
conspiring against them and the holiday season
fast approaching, Tanner and Olivia may just get
everything they want for Christmas after all!

*Available December 2008
wherever books are sold.*

HARLEQUIN® *Romance*®

Marry-Me Christmas

by *USA TODAY* bestselling author

SHIRLEY JUMP

A *Bride* FOR ALL *Seasons*

Ruthless and successful journalist Flynn never mixes
business with pleasure. But when he's sent to write a
scathing review of Samantha's bakery, her beauty and
innocence catches him off guard. Has this small-town
girl unlocked the city slicker's heart?

Available December 2008.

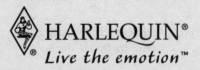

HARLEQUIN®
Live the emotion™

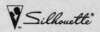

SPECIAL EDITION™

MISTLETOE AND MIRACLES

by *USA TODAY* bestselling author
MARIE FERRARELLA

Child psychologist Trent Marlowe couldn't believe his eyes when Laurel Greer, the woman he'd loved and lost, came to him for help. Now a widow, with a troubled boy who wouldn't speak, Laurel needed a miracle from Trent...and a brief detour under the mistletoe wouldn't hurt, either.

Available in December wherever books are sold.

THE MISTLETOE WAGER

Christine Merrill

Harry Pennyngton, Earl of Anneslea, is surprised when his estranged wife, Helena, arrives home for Christmas. Especially when she's intent on divorce! A festive house party is in full swing when the guests are snowed in, and Harry and Helena find they are together under the mistletoe....

*Available December 2008
wherever books are sold.*

Inside ROMANCE

Stay up-to-date on all your romance reading news!

The Inside Romance newsletter is a FREE quarterly newsletter highlighting our upcoming series releases and promotions!

Click on the <u>Inside Romance</u> link on the front page of **www.eHarlequin.com** or e-mail us at insideromance@harlequin.ca to sign up to receive your FREE newsletter today!

You can also subscribe by writing us at: HARLEQUIN BOOKS Attention: Customer Service Department P.O. Box 9057, Buffalo, NY 14269-9057

Please allow 4-6 weeks for delivery of the first issue by mail.

Coming Next Month

Season's greetings from Harlequin Romance®! Festive miracles, mistletoe kisses and winter weddings to get you into the holiday spirit as we bring you Christmas treats aplenty this month....

#4063 CINDERELLA AND THE COWBOY Judy Christenberry

With her two young children in tow, struggling widow Elizabeth stepped onto the Ransom Homestead looking for the family she'd never had. Despite being welcomed with open arms by the children's grandfather, it's blue-eyed rancher Jack who Elizabeth dreams will make their family complete....

#4064 THE ITALIAN'S MIRACLE FAMILY Lucy Gordon
Heart to Heart

Betrayed by their cheating partners, Alysa and Drago strike an unlikely friendship. But Alysa's calm facade hides a painful secret, which twists every time she sees Drago's child. Can the healing miracle of love make them a family?

#4065 HIS MISTLETOE BRIDE Cara Colter

Police officer Brody hates Christmas. Then vivacious Lila arrives in Snow Mountain and tilts his world sideways. But there's a glimmer of sadness in her soulful eyes. Until, snowbound in a log cabin, Brody claims a kiss under the mistletoe....

#4066 HER BABY'S FIRST CHRISTMAS Susan Meier

When millionaire Jared rescues Elise and her cute baby, Molly, and drives them home for the holidays, he finds himself reluctantly drawn to the tiny family. Elise secretly hopes that gorgeous Jared will stay for Molly's first Christmas—and forever!

#4067 MARRY-ME CHRISTMAS Shirley Jump
A Bride for All Seasons

A ruthless and successful journalist, Flynn never mixes business with pleasure. But when he's sent to write a scathing review of Samantha's bakery, her beauty and innocence catches him off guard. Has this small-town girl unlocked the city-slicker's heart?

#4068 PREGNANT: FATHER WANTED Claire Baxter
Baby on Board

There is more to Italian playboy Ric than he lets the world see. And pregnant travel writer Lyssa is determined to find out what. She's fiercely independent, but could Ric, in fact, be the perfect husband and father for her baby?

HRCNM1108